The Bobbsey Twins in a Great City

BY

LAURA LEE HOPE

AUTHOR OF "THE BOBBSEY TWINS," "THE BUNNY BROWN SERIES," "THE OUTDOOR GIRLS SERIES," ETC.

ILLUSTRATED

NEW YORK
GROSSET & DUNLAP
PUBLISHERS

Made in the United States of America

THE BOBBSEY TWINS IN A GREAT CITY

CONTENTS

THE BOBBSEY TWINS IN A GREAT CITY

CHAPTER I

THE ICE-BOAT

"OH, there comes my skate off again! Freddie, have you got any paste in your pocket?"

"Paste, Flossie! What good would paste be to fasten on your skate?"

"I don't know, but it might do *some* good. I can't make the strap hold it on any more," and a plump little girl shook back her flaxen, curling hair, which had slipped from under her cap and was blowing into her eyes, sat down on a log near the shore of the frozen lake and looked sorrowfully at the shining skate which had become loosened from her shoe.

"Come on, Flossie!" called the small, plump

boy, just about the size of his sister, and with her same kind of light hair and blue eyes. "There go Bert, Nan and Tommy Todd 'way ahead of us. We'll never catch up to 'em if you sit here. Come on!"

"I can't help sitting here, Freddie Bobbsey! How am I going to skate on only one skate?" asked the little girl.

"Put on the other, and come along."

"I have put it on, lots of times, but it comes off every time I skate a little bit. That's why I want some paste. Maybe I could paste the strap fast around my shoe."

"I don't believe you could, Flossie," and this time the small, plump boy stopped skating around in a ring—"grinding the bar," as it is called—and glided toward his sister seated on the log. "Anyhow, I haven't any paste. What made you think I had?"

"Oh, you carry so much stuff in your pockets I thought maybe you'd have paste."

"I might if it was summer, Flossie, and I was making kites with Bert. But I haven't any paste now."

"Then have you got a postage stamp?"

Helen Louise Solberg. Dec. 1925

L146172

From Dora & Ezra Rosenberg

"A postage stamp? Of course not! What good would a postage stamp be to fasten your skate strap?"

"Well, a postage stamp has paste on it, hasn't it? Anyhow, it's sticky, 'cause I got some on my tongue once, and I just know if I could only fasten down the end of this skate strap, to keep it from flopping up, and coming out of the buckle, I'd be all right. It's the flopping end that comes loose."

"Well, pooh! a postage stamp wouldn't be any good!" cried Freddie. "If you did stick it on it wouldn't last more than three strokes. A postage stamp wouldn't go far at all!"

"Some postage stamps do!" exclaimed Flossie. "Mother got one on a letter the other day and it had stuck itself on half-way round the world—she told me so. And if a stamp sticks half-way around the world I should think it would stick while I skated down to the end of the lake."

"Huh! That's different!" half grunted Freddie, for, just then, he was stooping over tightening one of his straps. "Anyhow, I haven't got a stamp."

"Well, maybe you could fix my skate so it wouldn't come off," suggested Flossie. "I've tried and tried, but I can't, and I don't want to stay here all alone."

"Why Flossie Bobbsey! I'm with you!"

"I know, but Nan and Bert are away down at the other end, with Tommy Todd, and Bert is going to buy hot chocolates. I know he is, 'cause he said so. I don't want to miss them."

"Me neither! Wait and I'll see if I can't fix your skate, Flossie."

Freddie was small—he and Flossie were the smaller pair of Bobbsey twins—but he was a sturdy little chap, and living out of doors, and playing games with his older brother Bert had taught Freddie how to do many things. He put Flossie's skate on her shoe, tightened the strap, and then made it still tighter by putting some pieces of wood under the leather loop.

"There!" he exclaimed, as he stood up, having been kneeling in the snow on the edge of the lake. "I guess that will hold, Flossie. Now come on, and we'll see how fast we can skate."

Together the brother and sister started off.

This time Flossie's skate seemed to be all right, needing neither paste nor a postage stamp to hold it on, and in a little while the smaller twins had caught up to Bert and Nan, their brother and sister, who, with a boy neighbor, named Tommy Todd, had slowed up to wait for them.

"What kept you?" asked Nan. "Did you try to do some fancy skating, Flossie?"

"I guess Freddie stopped to see if there wasn't a crack in the ice where he could get some water to play fireman," remarked Bert with a smile, for his small brother was very fond of this game, and his best-liked toy was a small fire engine, which, when a spring was wound, could squirt real water.

"No, I didn't stop at any cracks!" exclaimed Freddie earnestly. "Cracks in the ice is dangerous—Daddy said so. It was Flossie's skate."

"That's right—it kept coming off," explained the blue-eyed girl. "But Freddie fixed it, and he didn't have to use a postage stamp, either. Did you, Freddie?"

"Nope."

"Well, I guess they know what it means, but we don't!" laughed Nan, taking her small sister's hand. "Come on, now, you little twins. We waited for you, so we could all have hot chocolate together. You didn't get cold, I hope, stopping to fix your skate, Flossie?"

"Nope! I'm as warm as butter!"

"What does she mean by that?" asked Tommy Todd. "I often hear my grandmother say she's as warm as toast, but *butter*——"

"Well, when it's Winter, like it is now, you have to warm your butter so you can spread it on your bread," explained Flossie. "So I'm as warm as butter now."

"I wish I was!" cried Bert. "I'm getting a chill standing here waiting for you two! Come on, now. Skate lively, and we'll soon be there," and he pointed to a little candy and soda-water stand near the lower end of Lake Metoka, on the frozen surface of which the children were skating.

In the little cabin, which in Winter was built over the stand to make a warm place for skaters, hot chocolate and other drinks could be had, and Bert had promised to treat his brother and sisters, as well as Tommy Todd.

"Don't skate too fast," begged Flossie. "My skate *might* come off again, though Freddie fixed it pretty good."

"If it comes off again I'll skate and carry you on my back the rest of the way!" cried Bert. "I want something hot to drink. But mind you!" he cried, as he saw a mischievous look on his little sister's face, "don't dare make your skate come off on purpose! I don't want to carry you unless I have to."

"All right, Bert. I'll skate as fast as I can," promised Flossie.

The five started off, Tommy Todd skating beside Flossie to help her if she should need it. Tommy was a sort of chum of both pairs of twins, sometimes going with the older ones, Nan and Bert, and again with Flossie and Freddie. In fact, he played with these latter more often than with Nan and her twin, for Flossie and Freddie had played a large part in helping Tommy at one time, as I'll explain a little later.

It was a fine Winter's day, not too cold, and the sun was shining from a clear sky, but not warmly enough to melt the ice. The steel skates of the five children rang out a merry tune as they clicked over the frozen surface of the lake.

"Hurrah! Here we are!" cried Bert at last, as he skated on ahead and sat down on a bench in front of the "Chocolate Cabin," as they called the place. He began taking off his skates.

"Come on!" he called to the others. "I'll order the chocolate for you and have it cooling," for there was more trouble with Flossie's skate and Nan had stopped to help her fix it.

"Don't order chocolate for me, Bert!" called Nan. "I want malted milk. The chocolate is too sweet."

"Guess you're afraid of your complexion, Sis!" laughed Bert, as he went inside the little wooden house.

"Oh, Flossie, take both your skates off and walk the rest of the way," advised Nan, after she had tried, without much success, to fix the troublesome strap. "We'll get there sooner."

"All right," agreed Flossie. "It's a bother—this skate. I'm going to get a new pair."

"Maybe a new strap is all you need," said Tommy. "You can get one in there," and he nodded toward the little cabin.

A little later the five children were seated on stools in front of the counter, sipping the warm drinks which made their cheeks glow with brighter color and caused a deeper sparkle in their eyes.

"This is great!" cried Tommy Todd.

"That's what!" murmured Freddie, his nose deep in his cup.

"Don't forget about my strap," came from Flossie.

"Oh, yes," agreed Bert. "We don't want to have to drag you all the way home." The man who sold the chocolate and candy in the cabin also had skate straps for sale and one was soon found that would do for Flossie.

"Now my skate won't come off!" she cried, as once more they were on the ice. "I can skate as good as you, Freddie Bobbsey!"

"Let's have a race!" proposed Freddie. "Bert and Nan can give Flossie and me a head start, 'cause they're bigger than us. Will you?" he asked his brother.

"Yes, I guess so. A race will get us home quicker, and we're a little late."

"We'll let Flossie and Freddie start ahead of me," suggested Tommy, who, being a little older than the two smaller twins, was a little better skater.

"All right," agreed Bert. "Any way you like. Go ahead, Floss and Fred. Skate on until I tell you to wait. Then I'll give Tommy a starting place and, when we're all ready, I'll give the word to begin."

Flossie and Freddie, hand in hand, skated ahead a little way. But Freddie's skate went over a little piece of wood on the ice and he tripped and fell, pulling Flossie down with him. The two plump twins were in a heap on the ice.

"Hurt yourself?" asked Bert, as he started toward them, to help them up.

"No—no—I—I guess not," answered Flossie, who was the first to get up.

"We're all right," replied Freddie. "The ice was soft right there."

"I guess it's because they're so fat, that they're soft, like a feather pillow," laughed

Tommy. "They're getting fatter every day."

"That's what they are," agreed Nan with a smile. "But they are pretty good skaters for such small children."

"Everybody ready?" asked Bert, when the two small twins had taken their places, and Tommy Todd was between them and Bert and Nan.

"All right," answered Freddie.

"I am, too," came from Tommy.

"Then go!" cried Bert, suddenly.

The skating race was started. Merrily clicked the runners on the hard ice, leaving long white streaks where the children passed over. Flossie and Freddie were skating as fast and as hard as they could.

"They are very anxious to win," said Nan, who was skating beside her brother.

"Yes, but they can't keep going as fast as that all the way home."

"You're going to let them win, aren't you?" asked Nan.

"Sure I am! But they're so sharp we don't dare lag much behind. We must make a spurt toward the end, and pretend we did our best to beat them. Tommy Todd may come in ahead of them, though."

"We can skate up to him and tell him not to," suggested Nan.

"Good idea!" declared Bert. "We'll do it."

The older twins skated a little faster to overtake Tommy, who was some distance behind Flossie and Freddie, when suddenly Nan gave a cry and clutched Bert by the arm.

"Look!" she exclaimed, pointing with her hand.

"An ice-boat," remarked Bert. "And going fast, too!"

"Yes, but see! It's coming right toward Flossie and Freddie, and they're skating with their heads down, and don't see it! Oh, Bert! Yell at them! Tell them to look out! Yell at the man in the ice-boat!"

It did indeed seem a time of danger, for a swift ice-boat—one with big white sails and runners, like large skates under it, was skimming over the frozen lake straight for the smaller twins.

CHAPTER II

BUILDING THE "BIRD"

FLOSSIE and Freddie, anxious to win the skating race, were bending over with heads down, as all skaters do who wish to go fast and keep the wind from blowing on them too hard. So they did not see the ice-boat coming toward them, for the craft, blown by the wind, made hardly any noise, and what little it did make was taken up by the clicking of the skates of the smaller twins.

"Oh, Bert! Do something!" cried Nan.

"Yes, yes! I will—of course!"

Bert shook off Nan's hand, for it was still on his arm, and started to skate toward the twins as fast as he could. He hoped to reach them in time to stop them from skating right into the path of the oncoming ice-boat.

But he soon saw that he was not going to be able to do this. The ice-boat was coming toward the small twins faster than Bert could ever hope to skate and reach them.

"Yell at them!" shouted Nan. "That's the only way to stop them! Yell and tell them to look out!"

Bert himself had decided this was the best thing to do. He stopped skating and, making a sort of funnel, or megaphone, of his hands, he cried out:

"Flossie! Freddie! Look out! Danger—the ice-boat!"

Just at this moment, whether it was because of Bert's shouts or because they were tired of going so fast and wanted a rest, the two children leading the skating race stood up straight and looked back. They saw Bert pointing toward them and then they glanced at the ice-boat. It was very close, and Flossie screamed.

At the same time the man who was steering the boat saw the children. With a shout that echoed the one given by Bert, and the screams of Nan and Flossie, the man steered his boat to one side. But he made such a sudden change that, though he steered out of the way of Flossie and Freddie, he nearly ran into

Tommy Todd. That small boy, however, was a good skater and stopped just in time, for he had seen the ice-boat coming.

Then with a whizz and a clink of ice, as the runners of the boat scraped big chips from the frozen lake, the skimming boat shot past Nan and Bert, not doing a bit of harm, but scaring all five children very much.

"Sorry! Didn't see you! Next time——"

This was what the man in the ice-boat shouted as he whizzed by. His last words seemed whipped away by the wind and the children did not know what he meant.

"Maybe he meant next time he'd be sure to run into us," said Tommy Todd.

"Oh, he wouldn't do *that!*" declared Bert. "That was Mr. Watson. He buys lumber from my father. I guess he meant that next time he'd give us a ride."

"Oh, my!" exclaimed Nan. "Would you ride in one of those dangerous things, Bert Bobbsey?"

"Would I? Well, just give me the chance! How about you, Tommy?"

"I should say so! They're great!"

"Oh, I can't bear them!" went on Nan "Please let's stop and rest. My heart is beating so fast I can't skate for a while."

"All right—we'll call the race off," agreed Bert. Flossie and Freddie were a little startled by the closeness of the ice-boat, and they skated back to join their brother and sister.

And while they are taking a little rest on the ice I shall have a chance to let my new readers know something of the past history of the children about whom I am writing.

There were two pairs of Bobbsey twins. They were the children of Mr. Richard Bobbsey and his wife Mary, and the family lived in an Eastern city called Lakeport, which was at the head of Lake Metoka. Mr. Bobbsey was in the lumber business, having a yard and docks on the shore of the lake about a quarter of a mile from his house.

The older Bobbsey twins were Nan and Bert. They had dark hair and eyes, and were rather tall and slim. Flossie and Freddie, the younger twins, were short and fat, with light hair and blue eyes. So it would have been easy to tell the twins apart, even if one pair had not been older than the other. Besides the children and their parents there were in the "family" two other persons—Dinah Johnson, the fat, good-natured colored cook, and Sam, her husband, who looked after the furnace in the Winter and cut the grass in Summer.

Then there was Snoop, and Snap. The first was a fine black cat and the second a big dog, both great pets of the children. Those of you who have read the first book of this series, entitled "The Bobbsey Twins," do not need to read this explanation here, but others may care to. In the second volume I told you of the fun the twins had in the country. After that they went to the seashore, and this subject has a book all to itself, telling of the adventures there.

Later on the Bobbseys went back to school, where they had plenty of fun, and when they were at Snow Lodge there were some strange happenings, as there were also on the houseboat *Bluebird*. There was a stowaway boy—but there! I had better let you read the book for yourself.

The Bobbsey twins spent some time at Meadow Brook, but there was always a question whether they had better times there or "At Home," which is the name of the book just before this one.

You, who have read that book, will remember that Flossie and Freddie found, in a big snow storm, the lost father of Tommy Todd, a boy who lived with his grandmother in a poor section of Lakeport. And it was still that same Winter, after Tommy's father had come home, that we find the Bobbsey twins skating on the ice, having just missed being run into by the ice-boat.

"My! but that was a narrow escape!" exclaimed Nan, as she skated slowly about. "My heart is beating fast yet."

"So's mine," added Flossie. "Did he do it on purpose?"

"No, indeed!" exclaimed Bert. "I guess Mr. Watson wouldn't do a thing like *that!* He was looking after the ropes of the sail, or doing something to the steering rudder, and that's why he didn't see you and Freddie."

"What makes an ice-boat go?" asked Freddie.

"The wind blows it, just as the wind blows a sailboat," explained Bert, looking down the lake after the ice-boat.

"But it hasn't any cabin to it like a real boat," went on Freddie. "And it doesn't go in the water. Where do the people sit?"

"An ice-boat is like this," said Bert, and with the sharp heel end of his skate he drew a picture on the ice. "You take two long pieces of wood, and fasten them together like a cross—almost the same as when you start to make a kite," he went on. "On each end of the short cross there are double runners, like skates, only bigger. And at the end of the long stick, at the back, is another runner, and this moves, and has a handle to it like the rudder on a boat. They steer the ice-boat with this handle.

"And where the two big sticks cross they put up the tall mast and make the sail fast to that. Then when the wind blows it sends the ice-boat over the ice as fast as anything."

"It sure does go fast," said Tommy Todd. "Look! He's almost at the end of the lake now."

"Yes, an ice-boat goes almost as fast as the wind," said Bert. "Maybe some day——"

"Oh, come on!" cried Flossie. "I want to go home! I'm cold standing here."

"Yes, we had better go on," said Nan. "I'm all right now."

As the five children skated off, no longer thinking of the race, Nan asked Bert:

"What are you going to do some day?"

"Oh, I don't know. I haven't got it all thought out yet. I'll tell you after a bit."

"Is it a secret?" asked Nan, eagerly.

"Sort of."

"Oh, please tell me!"

"Not now. Come on, skate faster!"

Bert and Nan skated on ahead, knowing that Flossie and Freddie would try to keep up with them, and so would get home more quickly. But they did not leave the smaller twins too far behind.

A little later the Bobbseys were safe at home. Tommy Todd went to his grandmother's house, and Flossie and Freddie took turns giving their mother an account of their escape from the ice-boat.

"Was there really any danger?" asked Mrs. Bobbsey of Bert.

"Well, maybe, just a little. But I guess Mr. Watson would have stopped in time. He's a good ice-boat sailor."

"But don't let Flossie and Freddie get so far away from you another time. They might have been hurt."

Bert promised to look well after his little sister and brother, and then, having asked his mother if she wanted anything from the store, he said he was going down to his father's lumberyard.

"What for?" asked Nan, as she saw him leaving. "Is it about the secret?"

"Partly," answered Bert with a laugh.

Two or three days later the Bobbseys were again out skating on the ice, Nan and Bert keeping close to Freddie and Flossie. They had not been long gliding about when Freddie suddenly called:

"Oh, here comes that ice-boat again!"

"Surely enough, it is!" added Nan. "Oh, we must skate toward shore! Come on!"

"No need to do that," replied Bert. "It

isn't coming fast, and Mr. Watson sees us."

"He's waving his hand at us!" cried Flossie. "I guess he wants to give us a ride. Come on, Freddie!"

"Here! Wait a minute!" called Bert. "Don't get into any more danger. But I believe he *is* going to stop," he went on, as the ice-boat came slowly up to them. Then, as it swung up into the wind, with the sail loosely flapping, Mr. Watson called:

"Come on, children, don't you want to go for a ride?"

"Oh, let's!" cried Flossie, clapping her hands.

"And I want to steer!" added Freddie.

"No, you can't do that!" exclaimed Nan. "Oh, Bert, do you think it would be all right for us to go?" she asked her older brother.

"I don't see why not," said Bert. "The wind doesn't blow hard, and Mr. Watson knows all about ice-boats. I say let's go!"

"Oh, what fun!" cried Flossie and Freddie.

They took off their skates and walked toward the ice-boat. Mr. Watson smiled at them.

"I'm so sorry I nearly ran into you the other

day," he said. "I did not see you until almost the last minute. So I made up my mind the next time I saw you on the lake I'd give you a ride. Come on, now, get aboard!"

"He talks just as if it was a real boat!" laughed Flossie, for, living near the lake as they did, and often seeing boats at their father's lumber dock, the Bobbsey twins knew something about water craft.

"Well, of course, this isn't as big as some boats,' said Mr. Watson, "but it will hold all of us, I think."

The children saw where there was a sort of platform, with raised sides, built on the center of the crossed sticks, and on this platform were spread some fur rugs and blankets.

Mr. Watson saw to it that the little children, especially, were well wrapped, and then, telling them all to hold on, he let out the sail and away flew the ice-boat down the frozen lake, fairly whizzing along.

"My! how fa-fa-fast we go!" gasped Nan, for really the wind seemed to take away her breath.

"This sure *is* sailing!" cried Bert, and then

Nan noticed that her brother was looking at different parts of the ice-boat, as if to find out how it was made.

Flossie and Freddie were having lots of fun holding on to one another, and also to the sides of the ice-boat, for the craft slid this way and that so quickly, sometimes seeming to rise up in the air, that it was like being on the back of a horse.

But the Bobbseys liked it, and the ride in the ice-boat came to an end all too soon. With sparkling eyes, and red, glowing cheeks, the twins got out close to their father's lumber dock, calling their thanks to Mr. Watson.

"I'll take you again, some time," he answered, as he sailed off down the lake.

"Ah, ha! And so my little fat fireman had a ride in an ice-boat, did he?" cried Mr. Bobbsey that night, when he came home from the office and heard the story. "And how did my little fat fairy like it?" And he lifted up first Freddie and then Flossie to kiss them. "Fat fireman" and "fat fairy" were Mr. Bobbsey's pet names for the smaller twins. Bert and Nan had had pet names when they were small, but they were too large for them now, growing out of them as they grew out of their clothes.

"Oh, it was glorious!" cried Nan. "Sailing in an ice-boat must be like the way it feels to be in an airship."

"I'm going up in an airship when I get big!" cried Freddie, making a dive after Snoop, the cat, who was hiding under the table.

"Have you heard yet whether you are to go?" asked Mrs. Bobbsey, of her husband, when the noisy greetings to the children were over.

"No, not yet," he answered, and he made a motion with his head, as if to tell his wife not to speak of a certain matter before the children.

"Oh, I saw you wink!" cried Nan, clapping her hands. "What does it mean? Is it a secret, Momsey?"

"Well, yes, Nan. You shall be told in plenty of time, if anything comes of it."

"Oh, that's two secrets!" cried Nan. "Bert has one and now there's one here."

"What is Bert's secret?" asked Nan's mother.

"I don't know yet; he won't tell me."

"Yes, I'll tell you to-morrow," said her brother. "But what's this about Father going away, Mother? Are we going too?"

"Supper am ready, chilluns!" exclaimed the voice of Dinah, the cook, and that ended the talk about secrets for the time being.

"But when are you going to tell me *yours?*" Nan managed to whisper to her brother when the dessert was being served.

"Come down to the lumberyard to-morrow afternoon," he whispered. "It's almost done."

Without telling Flossie or Freddie anything about it, Nan slipped off by herself the next afternoon, and from the watchman in her father's lumberyard learned that Bert and another boy were in one of the sheds. As Nan came closer she could hear the noise of hammering and sawing.

"Oh, Bert, what are you making?" cried Nan, as she saw her brother and Tommy Todd busy with sticks, boards, hammer and nails.

"This is the *Bird!*" cried Bert, waving a hammer at something that, so far, did not look like much of anything.

"A bird?" cried Nan. "It looks more like a scare-crow!"

"Just wait until it's finished!" said Tommy Todd. "When we get the sail on——"

"Oh, Bert! is it a *boat?*" cried Nan eagerly.

"Yes, it's going to be an ice-boat, and I've called it the *Bird,*" was the answer. "I got the idea of building it after I'd seen Mr. Watson's. Father said I might, and he gave me the lumber, and let me have a carpenter to help, for Tommy and I couldn't do it all. But now the ice-boat is almost done and in a few days I'll sail it."

"And may I have a ride?" asked Nan.

"Of course. I'll take the whole family," said Bert. "Just you wait," and then he and Tommy went on hammering and sawing.

CHAPTER III

A RUNAWAY

"ALL aboard!"

"Don't forget your baggage!"

"This way for your tickets!"

"The ice-boat *Bird* makes no stops this side of the lake! All aboard!"

Bert Bobbsey and Tommy Todd thus were calling at the end of one of the lumberyard docks one day about a week after Nan had seen her brother building the ice-boat. Coming down the dock were Mr. and Mrs. Bobbsey, with Nan, Flossie and Freddie. Snap, the big dog, was bounding on ahead through the snow, barking joyously. He enjoyed fun as much as any one.

"All aboard! Please hurry up!" cried Bert.

"Why, I thought this was a *special* trip you were giving us, and we didn't have to hurry," laughed his mother.

"It is," Bert said. "But you see you can't sail an ice-boat if you haven't any wind, and I want you to have a ride before the wind dies away, as it might. So come on, get on board!"

"I want to steer!" cried Freddie.

"No, you must not," said Nan.

"Yes, I must. I know how to steer a motor boat, and I can steer an ice-boat, I guess," and Freddie was very sure about it.

"After a while, maybe," agreed Bert. "But an ice-boat is different to steer from a motor boat. I'll show you how, though."

Mr. and Mrs. Bobbsey got on the little platform which Bert had built as a sort of open cabin. It had old carpets and rugs on it, and there were blankets and robes to keep the passengers warm. After some failures Bert and Tommy had finally managed to finish the ice-boat. It was not as easy to build as they had expected, but Mr. Bobbsey's carpenter had helped them.

The boat had been tried out on the ice, and had sailed well. Mr. Bobbsey had Mr. Watson look at it, and that gentleman had said it was safe to ride in. Then Bert had finally gotten, his father and mother to promise to take a trip in the boat, bringing Nan, Flossie and Freddie with them. Mr. Bobbsey had, before this, been given a ride with Bert and Tommy, so he knew the two boys could manage the boat fairly well. Tommy and Bert had had several rides by themselves. Now they had company.

"Are you all ready?" asked Bert, after he had seen his father and mother, his sisters and brother, get on board the *Bird*.

"All ready," answered Mr. Bobbsey. "Don't go too fast at first, and take your mother's breath away."

"I won't!" promised Bert. "Are those two little ones covered up all right?" he asked, nodding toward Flossie and Freddie.

"Yep! We're as warm as—as popcorn!" cried Flossie.

"With butter on!" added Freddie.

"Well, you certainly ought to be good and warm," laughed Mrs. Bobbsey, as she tucked the robes closer around the two smaller twins.

"All aboard!" called Bert, and then, moving slowly at first, the ice-boat glided away from the lumber wharf, skimming over the lake with the entire Bobbsey family, not counting, of course, fat Dinah and her husband, who stayed at home. Nor was Snoop, the black cat, along. Snap, the dog, ran a little way, but when he found the ice-boat was going too fast for him, and when he noticed that he was slipping too much, he gave a sort of good-bye howl and went slowly back to shore.

"Isn't this great?" cried Bert, as he steered the ice-boat out into the middle of the lake.

"Wonderful!" cried Nan, her hair flying in the wind and her cheeks almost as red as roses. "I don't see how you made it, Bert."

"Well, it wasn't easy. How do you like it, Freddie?"

"All right. When can I steer?"

"Oh, maybe after a while," said Bert, with a laugh. "Say, we're going fast, all right."

"Yes," agreed Mr. Bobbsey. "I think the wind is getting stronger instead of dying out, Bert."

"It does seem so. Well, all the better. We won't have to walk back if it keeps on this way. We can sail to the end of the lake and ride back."

"Are you sure you can manage the boat yourself?" asked Bert's father. "She seems pretty big."

"Oh, Tommy and I sailed her in a stronger wind than this. And we have a heavier load on now, which makes it all the safer."

Mr. Bobbsey himself knew how to sail an ice-boat, but he wanted to let Bert do as much alone as he could, for this is a good way for a boy to learn, if there is not too much danger.

"And the worst that can happen," said Mr. Bobbsey, in a whisper to his wife, "is that we may upset and spill out."

"Oh! But do you really think there is any danger of *that?*"

"Well, there may be. Ice-boats often upset, but we can't fall very far," and he looked down at the ice, which was only a few inches below them. "And we have so many robes and blankets that falling would be like tumbling into bed. There is no danger."

The wind was blowing harder and harder. It was sweeping right across the lake and forcing the boat down. The steel runners clinked on the ice, now and then scraping up a shower of icy splinters that sparkled in the sun. On the other side of the lake were other ice-boats, and Bert wished he could have a race with some of them. But he knew his mother would not like that now.

"Can't you make it go a little slower?" asked Flossie, after a bit. "Every time I open my mouth it gets filled with cold air, and it makes me want to sneeze."

"I can't go any slower than the wind blows," answered Bert. "Turn your back to the bow, or front end of the boat, and you can open your mouth easier then."

Flossie did as she was told and felt better. Meanwhile the *Bird* was living up to her name, and skimming along swiftly. Bert held to the steering handle, now and then tightening or loosening the rope that was fast to the sail.

"Want any help?" asked his father.

"No, thank you, Dad. I want to manage it all by myself as long as I can."

"Isn't it my turn to steer?" asked Freddie, when they were half-way down the lake, toward the end farthest from the town, where there were deep woods on either side.

"No, not yet!" exclaimed Bert. "Don't touch anything, Freddie!" he went on, for his little brother was reaching out toward the sail. "I'll have to wait until the wind doesn't blow so strong before I can let your steer, Freddie."

"But I want to steer when we're going *fast!*" cried the little fellow. "I know how to do it. You just——"

Freddie never finished what he was saying. Whether he touched anything, or whether Bert was afraid he would, and so pulled on the wrong rope to keep it out of Freddie's way, was never known.

Suddenly the ice-boat gave a quick whirl to one side, like a boy or a girl on roller skates going around a corner. It went around so quickly that it tipped half-way over. Mrs. Bobbsey and Nan screamed. Mr. Bobbsey called to Bert to be careful, but it was too late. Bert had lost his hold of the rudder and the sail rope.

The next second Bert shot out of the ice-boat, and slid along on his back. A moment later his father and mother were also spilled out, followed by Nan. Then the ice-boat, not having such a heavy load aboard, settled down on the ice again, and started to run away, or, rather, blow away.

Right before the wind it flew, and Flossie and Freddie, being well tucked in among the robes and blankets were not spilled out. They stayed on board; and Mr. Bobbsey, sitting up after he had slid some distance across the ice, saw the *Bird* scooting down the lake, carrying his two smaller twins with it.

"Oh, the ice-boat is running away with Flossie and Freddie!" cried Nan, as she, too, saw what had happened.

CHAPTER IV

THE OLD WOODCHOPPER

WHILE Mr. and Mrs. Bobbsey, Bert and Nan picked themselves up from where they had fallen and slid along the ice, the ice-boat, with Flossie and Freddie snugly tucked in among the blankets and robes, was skimming down the lake, blown by a strong wind.

At first the two small twins hardly knew what had happened. They had felt the ice-boat tilt to one side, they remembered that they had nearly fallen out, and then they had sailed on again. It was not until Flossie opened her eyes (she always shut them when anything surprising was happening) that she saw she and Freddie were alone in the *Bird*.

"Why! Why!" she exclaimed. "Where are Daddy and Mother?"

"Yes, and Bert and Nan?" added Freddie. "Where is everybody?"

Then the two small twins looked back over the icy lake and far behind them saw their father and mother, with Bert and Nan, standing on the ice and waving their hands.

"Oh, they've jumped off and left us to sail the boat alone!" cried Freddie. "Now I can steer! Isn't that good?"

Flossie was not quite sure that this was "good," but, for a few seconds, she believed what Freddie had said— that the others had jumped off the ice-boat. She did not know that they had been spilled out, as Bert said afterward.

"Now watch me steer!" cried Freddie crawling back toward the tiller, which was the last thing Bert had let go of, as he shot from the boat.

"Oh, can you?" asked Flossie. "Do you think you can steer?"

"Of course I can," was the answer. "You just watch me. I'll make this boat go faster!"

"But you want to be awfully careful, Freddie."

"Oh, I'm always careful, ain't I?"

"Well, I s'pose you are—most times," answered Flossie, somewhat slowly. She did not wish to hurt her twin's feelings.

"Oh, I know what I'm doing," was Freddie's confident reply. "You just watch me! I'll make this boat go just as fast as anything!"

As it had happened, a rope had become caught around the tiller, or handle, of the rudder, thus holding it so that the ice-boat sailed straight before the wind. Otherwise it would have darted from side to side, and perhaps Flossie and Freddie would have been tossed out as the others had been. But it so happened that they sailed along nicely, no one being at the helm.

Straight down the lake sailed the *Bird* with the two little twins aboard. They had been a bit frightened at first, but now Freddie was thinking only of how he could steer the craft, and Flossie was waiting to see what her brother would do.

"I wonder what they're waving to us for?" asked Flossie, as she looked back and saw the frantic signals of her father and mother, Bert and Nan. "And they're running after us, too!" she added.

"Maybe they want us to come back," suggested Freddie. But as the ice-boat was too far away for the older Bobbseys to make their voices heard by Flossie and Freddie, Mr. Bobbsey and the others could only wave their hands.

"We must catch that boat!" cried Bert. "No telling what it will do to them if it upsets. Come on! Run, everybody!"

He set off as fast as he could go, his father with him, while Mrs. Bobbsey and Nan came along more slowly.

"I guess they want us to come back and get them," said Freddie. "They must be tired. Well, I'll steer the boat back and we'll give them a ride. Won't it be fun, Flossie?"

"Ye-yes, maybe. If you can do it."

"Do what?"

"Steer the ice-boat back."

"Of course I can do it!" cried Freddie. "I can squirt water from my fire engine, can't I? And that isn't any harder than this."

Freddie did not know so much about ice-boats as he thought he did, and when he had crawled back to the tiller, still held fast in a loop of the rope, the small boy found it harder to move than he had expected. Flossie stayed among the rugs and robes.

Freddie knew enough about boats to be sure that to steer one the tiller ought to move from side to side. So, finding that the rope, which was fast to the sail, was keeping the rudder handle from moving, he began to loosen the coils.

As soon as he did that the rudder moved from side to side, and this, of course, made the ice-boat do the same thing.

"Oh, dear!" cried Flossie, "don't jiggle it so, Freddie!"

"I—I can't—help it!" chattered Freddie, his words coming jerkily, for he was being "jiggled" himself, as the rudder shook from side to side in his hand. "This—this is the way to—to steer an ice-boat."

"Well, I don't like it," Flossie announced. "It makes me homesick!"

"Do you mean—*seasick?*" asked Freddie, trying his best to hold the tiller still.

"No, I mean homesick! I want to go home!"

"But we're having a nice ride, Flossie."

"I don't care! I want papa and mamma! I can't see them now!"

The ice-boat, sailing down the lake, had turned around a point of land, and this hid from view the rest of the Bobbsey family.

"I'll turn around and go back and get them," Freddie said. By this time he had taken the rope from the tiller, so the rudder handle moved freely from side to side. And then, all of a sudden, the *Bird* shot ahead more swiftly than before.

The wind was blowing more strongly, and when Freddie moved the rudder he steered the ice-boat so that the wind sent it straight ahead instead of a little to one side.

"Oh! oh!" cried Flossie, "this is too fast! How can we stop the ice-boat, Freddie?"

"I—I don't know," answered the little boy. "Don't you like to go fast, Flossie?"

"Not so fast as this. I can't make my nose work—I can't get any air!"

Indeed they were sailing even more swiftly than when Bert was steering, and Flossie was frightened. So was Freddie, but he was not so quick to say so.

"Please stop the boat!" cried Flossie again.

"Well, I'll try," promised Freddie. "I guess this is the rope you pull on," and he took hold of the one fast to the end of the sail—the rope that kept the big piece of white canvas from blowing away.

Freddie pulled on this, but it could not have been the right rope, or else he pulled it the wrong way, for, in an instant, the ice-boat seemed to "stand on its ear," as Bert spoke of it afterward. Flossie and Freddie were almost tossed out.

"Oh, don't do that!" cried the little girl.

"I—I didn't mean to," Freddie told her. "I guess I pulled on the wrong rope. Here's another. I'll try that."

By this time the ice-boat was more than two miles down the lake, for the wind was blowing hard and the *Bird* sailed swiftly. The children could not see their father, mother, Bert or Nan now. They would soon be at the end of the lake, and before them Flossie and Freddie could see big drifts of snow near the edge of the frozen lake and between it and the forest beyond.

"I—I guess we'd better stop pretty soon," faltered Freddie. "If we don't we'll run ashore."

With all his strength, he pulled on another rope, at the same time shoving the tiller over as far from him as it would go. The result was a surprise to him and to Flossie. The ice-boat turned quickly, and then, like a frightened horse, it darted toward shore.

Over the ice it skimmed. Then it turned up on one side, buried the bow, or front part, deep in a big snow drift and with another motion sent Flossie and Freddie, together with the robes and blankets, flying into a pile of soft snow. Down came the Bobbsey twins with a soft thud, not being in the least hurt.

For a moment neither of the children spoke. Then Flossie, brushing the snow from her face, looked around, and seeing Freddie near her, doing the same thing, she asked:

"What—what happened?"

"I guess I steered right up on shore instead of away from it," replied Freddie. "I must have turned the handle the wrong way. Are you hurt, Flossie?"

"Nope. Are you?"

"Nope. I hope the ice-boat isn't broken. Bert wouldn't like that. Let's go and look."

As the children floundered out of the snow, which had been left from a storm that had swept over the country before the lake had frozen, they heard a voice calling to them. Looking in the direction of the woods, they saw coming toward them an old man, wearing a big, ragged overcoat, a fur cap and mittens, while over his shoulder was an axe.

"Oh! oh!" said Flossie in a low voice. "Who—who's that, Freddie?"

"Oh, I know him. That's Uncle Jack, the woodchopper. He'll help us get the boat on the ice again, and I can sail it back home."

"Nope!" cried Flossie, shaking her flaxen curly head. "I'm never going to ride in an ice-boat with you any more. Never! You go too fast, and stop too quick. I'm going to *walk* home!"

"What's the matter, children?" asked Uncle Jack, and he came plowing his way through the snow. "Ah, your ice-boat is upset, I see! Well, you two are pretty small potatoes to be out sailing alone. 'Most froze, too, I'll warrant ye! Come on to my cabin. It's warm there, whatever else it is!" and he helped Flossie and Freddie from the snowdrift.

"Thank you," said Flossie. "But we're not potatoes, Uncle Jack."

"Well, little peaches, then. Anyhow, your cheeks look like red apples," said the man, laughing.

CHAPTER V

GLORIOUS NEWS

"How did it all happen?" asked Uncle Jack, a little later, as he led Flossie and Freddie along a path through the snow to his cabin in the woods. "Why are you two out ice-boating alone?"

"The rest of 'em spilled out," answered Freddie; "and I upset Flossie and me when I pulled on the wrong rope. But we're not hurt a bit. It was fun. Wasn't it, Flossie?"

"Ye—yes, I—I guess so."

"Hum! You're part of the Bobbsey twins, aren't you?" asked the old woodchopper, who made a living by cutting firewood and kindling wood in the forest, where he lived by himself in a lonely cabin all the year around.

"Yes, we're the littlest ones," answered Flossie. "Bert and Nan are bigger, but they fell off, too."

"So falling from an ice-boat doesn't go by sizes," laughed the old man.

Then, taking turns, Flossie and Freddie told the story of the runaway ice-boat, and of having left the rest of their family several miles away on the ice.

"We tried to stop, but we couldn't," said Flossie. "And, oh, dear! I wonder where Daddy and Mother are now." Flossie spoke as though it would not take much to make her cry.

"Don't worry," said Uncle Jack, as every one around Lakeport called him. "If your father and mother don't come for you I'll take you home."

"It—it's a long way to walk," said Freddie with a sigh. "And I guess Flossie is hungry. Aren't you?" he asked of his little sister.

"Well—a little," admitted the blue-eyed girl twin.

"How about you, little man?" asked Uncle Jack.

"I—I guess I am, too," Freddie admitted. "Have you got anything to eat?"

"Well, maybe we can find something in my

cabin," said the old man. He had left his axe sticking in a tree near where the ice-boat had run into the snow bank, and was leading the children along by either hand. Flossie and Freddie looked up into his kindly, wrinkled face, the cheeks glowing red like two rosy apples, and they knew they would be well taken care of. Uncle Jack was a fine, honest man, and he was always kind to children, who, often in the Summer, would gather flowers near his lonely log cabin.

In a little while Flossie and Freddie were seated in front of a stove, in which crackled a hot fire, eating bread and milk, which was the best the woodchopper could offer them. But they were so hungry that, as Freddie said afterward, it tasted better than chicken and ice-cream.

"Haven't you got any little girl?" asked Flossie after a while.

"No, I haven't a chick or a child, I'm sorry to say."

"My father would give you a chicken if you wanted it," said Freddie. "And some days *we* could come and stay with you."

"That last part would be all right," said the old man with a smile; "but I haven't any place to keep a chicken. It would get lonesome, I'm afraid, while I'm off in the forest chopping wood. But I thank you just the same."

"Didn't you ever have any children?" asked Flossie, taking a second glass of milk which the kindly old man gave her.

"Never a one. Though when I was a boy I lived in a place where there were two children, I think. But it's all kind of hazy."

"Where was that?" asked Freddie, brushing up the last of the bread crumbs from his plate.

"I don't remember much about my folks. Most of my life has beent spent working on farmers' land, until I got so old I could not plow or cut hay. Then the man who owns this forest said I might come here and chop firewood, and I did. I built this cabin myself, and I've lived all alone in it for many years."

This was so, for Jack had been in the woods from the time when Bert and Nan were babies, so Flossie and Freddie had often heard their older brother and sister say.

"Haven't you any folks?" asked Freddie.

"Well, I seem to remember that once I had a brother and a sister. But I lost track of them, and they lost me, I guess; so where they are now, if they're anywhere, I don't know. I'm all alone, I guess," and the woodchopper's face was sad.

"Never mind! We'll come to see you," said Flossie, with a smile. "But now maybe we'd better start home, Freddie. Papa and Mamma may be worried about us."

"I'll take you home, if you've had enough to eat," said Uncle Jack.

"Oh, we've had plenty, thank you," said Freddie. "But it's a long way to go home. If I could sail the ice-boat back——"

"I don't like that boat!" cried Flossie.

"How would you like to ride on a sled?" asked the woodchopper. "In a sled drawn by a horse with jingling bells?"

"That would be *fine!*" cried Freddie, clapping his hands. "But where is he—the horse, I mean?"

"Oh, out in my little stable. I built a small stable, as well as this cabin, for I have to haul my wood into town to sell it. I'll get my bobsled ready and tuck you in among the blankets that spilled from your ice-boat. Then I'll drive you home."

Flossie and Freddie liked this plan, and were soon snugly tucked in among their own robes, for the ice-boat had upset not far from the woodchopper's cabin.

"Your folks will likely be worried about you," said Uncle Jack, "so I'll get you home as fast as I can, though my horse isn't very speedy. He's getting old, like myself."

"You don't *look* old," said Flossie kindly.

"Well, I am. I'm old and full of pains and aches."

"Have you got a stomachache?" asked Flossie. "If you have my mother could give you some peppermint."

"My pain is in my bones and back; peppermint isn't much good for that. I guess I need to go to a hospital. But never mind me, I must look after you children now."

Along through the snow jogged the woodcutter's horse, his bells jingling as he hauled the sled over the road that led along the shore of the lake.

"What'll we do about Bert's ice-boat?" asked Flossie.

"I'll look after it until he comes for it," said Uncle Jack. "It isn't damaged any, and it will be all right. Few folks come down to this end of the lake in Winter. I have it all to myself."

"You must be lonesome," remarked Freddie.

"I am, sometimes. Often I wish I had folks, like other men. But it isn't to be, I reckon. G'lang there, Bucksaw."

"Is that the name of your horse?"

"Yes. Bucksaw is his name. Pretty good for a woodchopper's horse, I guess," and the old man smiled.

While Flossie and Freddie were being driven home by the woodchopper, Mr. and Mrs. Bobbsey, with Bert and Nan, left far behind on the ice when the *Bird* upset, were much worried and excited.

"What can we do?" cried Bert.

"We must go after those children!" exclaimed Mrs. Bobbsey.

"That's what I'm going to do," Mr. Bobbsey remarked.

"If I could borrow one of those ice-boats over there," put in Bert, pointing toward some on the other side of the lake, "I could sail down and get them."

"No more ice-boats to-day!" said Mrs. Bobbsey. "Oh, I do hope nothing happens to Flossie and Freddie!"

"I don't believe they'll be hurt," said their father. "Even if they fall out they can't get much of a bump on the ice, and if they run ashore, as they're likely to do, they'll only fall in the snow. Don't worry."

"But we *must* go after them!" cried his wife.

"Just what I am going to do. Bert and I will go to shore, hire a team and drive down the lake after them. The road runs right along the lake shore and we'll be sure to see them, or hear something of them. They'll be all right."

It did not take Mr. Bobbsey and Bert long to get started on the search for the missing ones, for Flossie and Freddie in the ice-boat had sailed around the point of land, as I told you, and were out of sight of their folks.

Mrs. Bobbsey and Nan were taken home by

some friends who happened to pass the lake in their automobile, and half-way to the woodcutter's cabin, though he had no idea the children had been there, Mr. Bobbsey and Bert met them being driven to Lakeport by Uncle Jack.

"Oh, there's Daddy!" cried Freddie.

"And Bert!" added Flossie, as she saw her brother. "Your ice-boat's all right," she added. "We just fell out of it."

"Are *you* all right?" asked Mr. Bobbsey, stopping his horses.

"Fine!" cried Freddie. "And we had bread and milk."

"Well, I'm sure I'm much obliged to you, Uncle Jack," said the children's father. "It was very kind of you."

Then Flossie and Freddie told their story, and the woodchopper told of having seen them tossed into the snow and of how he helped them out, and then Mr. Bobbsey told what had happened to him, the children's mother, Bert and Nan.

"I just pulled on the wrong rope, that's all, and I guess I steered the boat crooked," said Freddie with a laugh.

"You're lucky it was no worse," remarked Bert, laughing also. "But as long as you two are all right, and the *Bird* isn't damaged, I'm glad."

Mr. Bobbsey was also, and then he took the children into his sleigh, driving home with them while Uncle Jack turned back.

"I like him," said Flossie, speaking of the old woodchopper to her father. "He hasn't a chick or a child and he lives all alone in the woods."

"Yes, poor Uncle Jack doesn't have a very happy life," said Mr. Bobbsey. "I must see what we can do to help him."

Little was talked of in the Bobbsey home that afternoon and evening but the adventure with the ice-boat, and what had happened to Flossie and Freddie when it ran away with them.

The next day Bert and Tommy Todd got the *Bird* back and had fine times sailing in it. Flossie and Freddie, as well as some of their friends, were also given rides, but Bert cut the sail smaller so his boat would not go so fast, making it safer.

When the Bobbsey twins were not ice-boating they were skating, or building snow forts or snow men. Once Flossie and Freddie built a little snow house and got inside it with Snoop, the black cat, and Snap, the dog.

Everything was very nice, but the house was so small that, when they were all in it, there was not room for Snap to wag his tail. And as there never was a dog yet, with a tail, who did not want to wag it, you can easily guess what happened.

Either Snap wagged his tail in the faces of Flossie and Freddie or he whacked Snoop with it, and as the cat did not like that she ran out of the snow house.

But Snap kept on wagging his tail, and as Flossie and Freddie made him get to one side when he did it the only other place he had to wag it was against the sides of the snow house.

Now these snow sides were not very thick or strong—they were not made to be wagged against by a big dog's tail, and, all of a sudden, Snap wagged his tail right through the snow house.

Then, with a swish and a swush, down the snow house toppled right on the heads of Flossie, Freddie and Snap. Snap gave a howl and dug his way out. But the two small twins were laughing so hard that it took them a little longer to dig their way out.

They were not hurt in the least, however, and they thought it great fun to have the snow house fall on them when Snap's tail wagged too hard.

It was about a week after the funny iceboat ride that Mr. Bobbsey came home from his office a little earlier than usual. He was smiling, and when his wife saw him she asked:

"Did it come?"

"Did what come?" asked Nan. "Are we going to have a new automobile, Mother?"

"Not yet, Nan."

"Then what came?"

"Glorious news!" cried her father, catching her up and kissing her. "Glorious news came in a letter. We are all going to a great city!"

"To live?"

"No, just on a visit," said Mrs. Bobbsey. "Oh, it is good news! I have been wanting to go for a long while. Come in, Bert—and you too, Flossie and Freddie—and hear the good news!" she called to the other twins. "Daddy has glorious news for us!"

CHAPTER VI

ON TO NEW YORK

"Are we going?" cried Flossie, when she heard that the family was about to make some sort of a journey.

"And can we take the ice-boat?" Freddie asked eagerly.

"Yes, of course you're going," said Mrs. Bobbsey.

"But no ice-boat," added Bert. "There's no chance to sail one in New York City—and if there was we wouldn't have time."

"Oh, are we going to New York?" cried Flossie.

"Yes," her father nodded.

"Then I'm going to take my fire engine!" cried Freddie. "They have fires in New York, don't they, Daddy?"

"Plenty of them, I think. And they have big engines there to put them out—larger ones than we have in Lakeport. But now let's get quiet so I can tell Mother and you the news."

Then, with the smaller twins cuddled up on his lap and Bert and Nan seated near their mother, Mr. Bobbsey told the news. He was going to start a new business, from which he hoped to make a great deal of money, and he had to go to New York to see about it. The trip would take the best part of a day from Lakeport, and Mr. Bobbsey would have to stay in the big city several weeks.

He had long promised his wife that when the time came to go to New York he would take her and the whole family with him, and that time had now come.

"When can we start?" Flossie inquired.

"To-night?" asked Freddie eagerly.

"Oh, indeed not!" laughed his mother. "It will take at least a week to get ready, and perhaps longer. You children have to have some new clothes, and Daddy has to look after his business here. I think we will close this house, and Dinah and Sam can visit their friends."

"What about Snap and Snoop?" asked Flossie.

"Oh, let's take them!" begged Freddie.

"It would be no fun going to New York with pet cats and dogs," said Bert. "They'd only be in the way or get lost."

"I wouldn't want either one of 'em to get lost," put in Flossie.

"Then we'll leave them with Dinah," said Mother Bobbsey, glad that that part was over. Every time they went away it was always hard to get the younger twins to consent to leave Snoop and Snap at home.

"It will be great, going to New York!" cried Bert. "I want to see some of the flying machines I've read about."

"And I want to see some of the lovely stylish dresses the girls wear as they ride on Fifth Avenue," declared Nan. "Mother, do you think I could have a *real* dress from New York?" she asked in a whisper. "Not one that's *too* stylish, of course, but so I could say it came from New York."

"I guess so," and Mrs. Bobbsey smiled. "But let's hear what Flossie and Freddie most want to see in New York," and she looked at the two small twins.

Flossie and Freddie thought for a moment, and then the blue-eyed boy, shaking his flaxen curls, cried:

"I want to see a big fire, and watch the firemen put it out. But I hope nobody gets hurt!"

"That last part is good, anyhow," said Mr. Bobbsey. "And how about my little fat fairy?" and he playfully pinched Flossie's plump leg. "What do you want to see?"

Flossie did not answer at once, but when she did she cried:

"A monkey!"

"A monkey?" repeated her father.

"Yes, the monkeys in the park. I read about them, and how they do such funny tricks in their cages. That's what I want to see—the monkeys in the park."

"Oh, so do I!" cried Freddie. "Can I see the monkeys and a fire too?"

"Well, I guess so," answered his father. "But we will hope no big fires will occur while we are in New York. As for monkeys, I guess there will be plenty of them in the park."

The children were so excited, thinking about

the trip to the great city of New York, they could hardly sleep that night, even though they stayed up later than usual.

And the next day a busy time began. Mrs. Bobbsey had to see to getting ready the clothes for herself and the children. At this Nan helped some, but Flossie and Freddie could not, for they were too small. Bert ran on a number of errands for his father, before and after school, for the children had their lessons to do even while getting ready for the trip.

Of course they could not go to school in New York very well, but Mr. Bobbsey arranged with the teachers in Lakeport that the twins could make up, when they came back, any lessons they should miss. And as Nan and Bert were ahead of their class, and as Flossie and Freddie were only in the "baby" grade, where they did not have hard lessons, as yet, staying from school would do not great harm to any of them.

But at last all was ready for the start. The trunks and valises had been packed, the children had said good-bye to their many friends and playmates, Dinah and Sam had gone away and the dog and cat had been sent to board near the cook's home until the Bobbseys should come back.

Mr. Bobbsey had left his business with his partner to look after, and Bert had said Tommy Todd could sail the ice-boat as much as he pleased while Bert was in New York.

"Well, I guess we're ready to start," said Mr. Bobbsey, when the house had been locked and the big automobile that was to take them to the station was puffing out in front. "All aboard!"

"This isn't the train, Daddy!" laughed Nan.

"No, but we'll soon be there," her father answered. "Come along."

Into the automobile they piled, parents, twins, baggage and all, and off they started. On the way to the depot Flossie cried:

"Oh, there's Uncle Jack!" and the sled of the woodchopper was seen moving slowly down the village street, with a load of logs piled high on it.

"Poor old man," murmured Mrs. Bobbsey. "Did you see if you could help him in any way?" she asked her husband.

"Yes, I have arranged it so that Uncle Jack

will have plenty of food this Winter. He can keep warm, for he has a stove and can cut all the wood he wants. I sent our doctor to see him. But Dr. Haydon thinks Uncle Jack should go to a hospital."

"Then why don't you send him? He was so good to the children——"

"I know he was, but he won't go to the hospital. He says he knows it costs money and he won't let me spend any on him. But when I come back from New York I'll see what I can do. I think he'll be all right for a while, poor old man."

Uncle Jack, sitting on top of his load of wood, saw the children in the automobile and waved to them. The Bobbsey twins waved back.

"We must bring him something from New York," said Freddie.

"We could get him a little toy chick, and then he wouldn't be lonesome. Maybe he'd like that," added Flossie.

Little did the two small Bobbsey twins think what they would help to bring back from New York for the poor, old woodchopper.

The train for New York was on time, and soon the twins, each pair in one seat, with Father and Mother Bobbsey behind them, were looking out of the car windows, happy and joyous as they started on their journey.

They were on their way to the great city of New York.

I shall not tell you all that happened on the trip. It was not really much, for by this time the twins had traveled so often that a railroad train was an old story to them. But they never tired of looking out of the windows.

On and on clicked the train, rushing through the snow-covered country, now passing some small village, and again hurrying through a city.

Now and then the car would rattle through some big piece of woods, and then Flossie and Freddie would remember how they were tossed out of the ice-boat, and how they had been so kindly cared for by Uncle Jack in his lonely log cabin.

It was late in the afternoon when, after a change of cars, the Bobbsey family got aboard a Pennsylvania railroad train that took them over the New Jersey meadows. They crossed two rivers and then Flossie and Freddie, who were eagerly looking out of the windows, suddenly found themselves in darkness.

"Oh, another tunnel!" cried Freddie.

"Is it, Daddy?" asked Flossie.

"Yes, it's a big tunnel under the Hudson River. In a little while you will be in New York."

And not long afterward the train came to a stop. The children found themselves down in a sort of big hole in the ground, for the Pennsylvania trains come into the great Thirty-third Street station far below the street.

Up the steps walked the Bobbsey family, red-capped porters carrying their hand-baggage, and, a little later, Flossie, Freddie and the others stood under the roof of the great station in New York. They were in the big city, and many things were to happen to them before they saw Lakeport again.

CHAPTER VII

ON THE EXPRESS TRAIN

Mr. Bobbsey wished to ask one of the railroad men in the big station some questions about the trunks, and he also had to send a telegram, so, while he was doing these things, he told his wife and children to sit down and wait for him. Mrs. Bobbsey led Nan and Bert and Flossie and Freddie to one of the many long benches in the large depot, but the two smaller twins were so excited at being in such an immense place that they had not been seated more than a few seconds before they jumped up to gaze all about them. Bert and Nan, too, though older than their brother and sister, were much astonished at what they saw.

"Why—why!" gasped Freddie, "it's bigger than our armory at home!" for in Lakeport there was a big hall where the soldiers drilled.

"It's three times as big," said Flossie.

"Four!" declared Freddie. "Come on!" he called to his sister, "let's see how long it takes to walk around it."

"Don't go too far away," said Mrs. Bobbsey, who, for the moment, did not realize how really large the station was. "Don't get lost!" she went on.

"No'm, we won't!" promised Flossie and Freddie.

They started off to walk around the large depot, which, as you who have seen it know, takes up a whole New York City block, or "square," as you will say if you live near Philadelphia.

Mr. Bobbsey's business took him a little longer than he expected, but as Bert and Nan begged to be allowed to buy a little candy at the newspaper stand near them, and as Mrs. Bobbsey wanted a magazine, the getting of these things took a little time, so the three did not notice how long Mr. Bobbsey was away from them.

When he came back, having sent his message and found out what he wanted to know, the twins' father asked:

"Where are Flossie and Freddie?"

"They're walking around, just seeing how big the station is," said Nan.

"Trying to find out how much larger it is than our armory at home," added Bert with a laugh.

"Well, I hope they don't get lost," said Mr. Bobbsey. "This place is a good deal larger than our armory. I'd better go to look for them," he went on as a glance around, near the news stand, did not show the two little ones anywhere in sight.

"I'll come with you," offered Bert.

"No, you'd better stay here with your mother," said his father. "I don't want you getting lost, too." And he smiled at his son. "Stay right here. I'll not be long."

But if Mr. Bobbsey thought he was going to find Flossie and Freddie soon he was disappointed. He wandered about under the big glass roof, which at first the two younger twins had taken for the sky; but he did not see Flossie or Freddie.

"Has yo'all done lost suffin, boss?" inquired one of the colored porters.

"I'm looking for my two little children," explained Mr. Bobbsey. "They wandered away from their mother."

"Oh, don't yo'all worry 'bout *dat,* boss! Chilluns gits lost heah ebery day, an' we all easy find 'em ag'in."

"Oh, I'm not worried," answered Mr. Bobbsey, with a smile. "But it is time for us to go, and I want them. Did you see them—two little ones—about so high," and he held his hand a short distance above the stone floor. "They have light hair and blue eyes."

The porter thought for a moment. Then he said:

"Well, to tell yo' de truff, boss, we has about seben hundred blue-eyed an' light-haired chilluns in heah ebery day, and we has de same number ob dark ones, so it's mighty hard t' 'member 'em all."

"Yes, I suppose so. Well, I'll walk about. I dare say I shall find them."

"I'll tell some ob de udder men," offered the porter. "We often has t' pick up lost little ones an' take 'em to de waitin' room. Ef yo' doan't find yo' tots yo'se'f, stop in dere."

"I will," said Mr. Bobbsey, and he was about to walk on when the porter called to him:

"Heah comes a light-haired, blue-eyed gal now, an' she's runnin' like she's in a hurry. Maybe she's yo'rs."

Mr. Bobbsey looked up in time to see Flossie running toward him from the front part of the station. She seemed much excited, and when she neared her father she called:

"Oh, Daddy! guess what happened!"

"I'm afraid I haven't time," said Mr. Bobbsey quickly. "We must hurry away. Where is Freddie?"

"That's what I mean! Guess what happened to him," went on Flossie, who was rather out of breath.

"I can't," said Mr. Bobbsey. "Tell me quickly, Flossie. Is he hurt?"

"Oh, no; he's all right. But he's gone off down the street, and he went into a store where there was a lot of bugs in the window, and he says he's going to buy some. I want some bugs, too!"

"What in the world is she talking about?" asked Mrs. Bobbsey, who from where she sat had seen her husband and little girl and had hurried on to join them.

"She says Freddie went down the street," explained Mr. Bobbsey, "and that he——"

"Yep! He went in a store with a lot of bugs in the window!" said Flossie again. "They're great big bugs and they walk around and around and around!" and she shook her flaxen head as hard as she could, as she often did when excited.

"What in the world do you mean?" asked Nan, who, with Bert, now joined their father.

"Freddie must have gone outside the depot to go down a street," said Bert. "Maybe she means he went into an animal store, where they sell monkeys and parrots."

"No, they weren't any monkeys—nor parrots, either," said Flossie. "But some of the big bugs were green like a parrot. And we didn't go outdoors, either."

"Then show us where you did go," ordered Mr. Bobbsey quickly. "I think we can find Freddie that way. Did you go into the store with him?" he asked his little girl.

"Nope. I ran back to get the money to buy

the bugs that crawl around and around and around, and go in a little door all by theirselves!" said Flossie, who was not breathing so fast now.

"What is it all about?" asked Mrs. Bobbsey. "We seem to have found a queer part of New York as soon as we arrive."

"It's over this way," and Flossie, taking her father's hand, pulled him in the direction from which she had come. Up a flight of broad stone steps she led him, the others following, until, as they approached the main entrance of the station, Flossie pointed and said:

"There's the street with all the stores on it. Freddie went down there, and we stopped in front of a window where the bugs are, that go around and around and——"

"Yes, dear, we know all about how they go around," said her mother, with a smile. "But show us where Freddie is."

"Just down the street," said Flossie. "Come on."

"Oh, I see what she means!" exclaimed Mr. Bobbsey. "It's the arcade. This is part of the depot—the vestibule, so to speak," he went on,

"It's the entrance, and it is so big that there is room for stores on either side. It does look like a street."

And so it did, except that there were no automobiles or wagons in it—just people hurrying along. On either side of the arcade were stores, where fruit, candy, toys, flowers and other things were sold. You can imagine that a station which has room in it for many trains, automobiles and thousands of people easily has room for stores also.

"Come on—right down this way!" called Flossie, hurrying ahead of the others. "I'll show you where the bugs are."

"The bugs that go around and around and around," laughed Bert, in a low tone to Nan.

"Oh, I do hope Freddie hasn't gotten into any trouble," sighed Nan, who, though she was only ten years old, felt much more grown up than either Flossie or Freddie.

"Here are the bugs!" cried Flossie, a little later, and she stopped in front of a station toy store, in the window of which a young man was showing how big tin bugs would move along on a spring roller that was fastened beneath them. There were green, red, yellow and spotted bugs, and they did indeed go "around and around and around," as Flossie had said, and some of them steered themselves, when started by the young man, into the door of a little pasteboard house, where all the toy tin bugs seemed to live.

"There's Freddie now, buying a bug!" cried Flossie, as she saw through the store door her brother talking to a clerk. And the clerk was showing Freddie how the bug "walked" on the wooden roller which answered for legs.

"I want a bug, too!" Flossie cried, and into the store dashed the little girl. "I've brought back Papa and Mamma and Bert and Nan," Flossie explained to her brother. "They all want to see the bugs."

"Well!" exclaimed the man in the store. "This is going to be a busy day for me, I guess," and he smiled at the Bobbsey family.

"Can I have three of these bugs, Daddy?" asked Freddie, just as if he had caused no trouble at all by going off as he had done.

"I want three, too," echoed Flossie.

"Oh, what funny looking things!" cried Mrs.

Bobbsey, as the clerk sent the bugs crawling "around and around."

"They are very amusing," said the salesman, "and just the thing for children. They can play many games with them and keep out of mischief."

"They'll have to be pretty good to keep *these* youngsters out of mischief," said Mr. Bobbsey, with a smile. "Yes, Freddie, you may have some bugs, and Flossie also. How about you, Nan and Bert?"

"I'd rather have that small aeroplane," said Bert, pointing to one that could be wound up with a rubber band and would fly for some distance.

"And I'd like that work basket," said Nan.

"Well, we'll get you all something, and then we must start for our hotel," said Mr. Bobbsey. "Come, Freddie, pick out the bugs you want, and don't run away again. You might get lost, even if you are only in the railroad station."

"I couldn't get lost—Flossie knew where I was," said Freddie. "I sent her back to bring you, so you could pay for my bugs."

Then the two younger Bobbseys looked over about all the toy tin bugs in the station store, and finally picked out those they wanted, though it took some little time. Bert's and Nan's gifts were wrapped up long before Freddie could make up his mind whether to take a blue bug, striped with green, or a purple one, spotted with yellow, finally making up his mind that the last was best.

Then, after all the baggage had been collected, the family was ready to start for the hotel where they were to stay while in New York. Mr. Bobbsey wanted to get a taxicab, but Flossie and Freddie had heard of the elevated trains, which ran "in the air," and they wanted to go in one of them, saying it would be such fun. So, as it was almost as near one way as it was the other, Mr. Bobbsey consented, and they set off for the elevated railroad.

"Oh, there goes a train!" cried Flossie, as they came in sight of the station, which was high above the street, set on iron pillars, some of which also held up the elevated track. "Just think, Freddie, we're going to ride on a high train!" Flossie was quite excited.

"I hope it doesn't fall," said Nan.

"They're made strong on purpose, so they won't fall," said Bert.

Flossie and Freddie ran on ahead up the elevated stairs, and just as their father was buying the tickets, to drop in the little box where the "chopper" stood, working up and down a long handle, a train rumbled into the station.

The iron gates of the car platforms were pulled back, several persons hurried off and others hurried on. Flossie and Freddie, thinking this was the train their parents, Bert and Nan, were going to take, and, being anxious to get seats near the window where they could look out, rushed past the ticket chopper, darted through the open gates and into one of the cars.

CHAPTER VIII

A LONG RIDE

FLOSSIE and Freddie, scurrying through the gates of the elevated car just as the guard was about to close them, saw inside two rows of seats on either side, there being very few passengers in that coach. Thinking their father and mother, with Bert and Nan, were right behind them, the two little twins felt no fear, but rushed in, each one anxious to get a seat.

"I'm going to sit by a window!" cried Freddie.

"So'm I!" added Flossie, and both were soon kneeling on the rattan seats, with their noses fairly flattened against the glass of the window. The few passengers in the train smiled, for they knew the children must be from somewhere outside of New York, as the little folk of that city are not so eager to see the sights amid which they live.

It was not until the train had started, and had gone several blocks, that Flossie and Freddie thought of their father and mother. They were greatly interested in looking out of the windows, and watching the train rush past at the level of the upper stories of the houses and stores along the streets. It did seem so queer to them to be riding in a train high up in the air, instead of on the ground.

"It's lots better than a tunnel, and I used to think they were lots of fun!" said Flossie, fairly bubbling over with joy.

"It's great!" cried Freddie, and he flattened his nose out more than ever against the glass, trying to look around a corner. For he had seen in one window of a house a boy dropping from the window of his home a basket on a string, and Freddie wanted to see why he was doing this.

It is no unusual sight in New York, to see children, not much larger than the small Bobbsey twins, traveling about alone, so the other passengers and the trainmen, after the first few smiles, paid no attention to Flossie and Freddie. But the two themselves, after their first wonder at the sights they saw, began to think of their father and mother, as well as of Bert and Nan.

"Where are they?" asked Flossie, after a bit, as she turned around and sat down in her seat.

"Didn't they—didn't they come in after us?" asked Freddie, his chubby face taking on a worried look.

"I—I didn't see them," returned Flossie. "Maybe they're in another car. Let's go to look!"

To say a thing was generally to do it, with the smaller Bobbsey twins, at least, and no sooner did Flossie say this than Freddie was ready to go with her on a hunt for the others. The children slipped from their seats and started for the door while the train was moving swiftly, but a guard, who is a sort of brakeman, stopped them.

"Where are you youngsters going?" he asked good-naturedly.

"We want our father and mother," explained Freddie. "They must be in another car. We hurried on ahead."

"Well, it wouldn't be the first time that has

happened," said the guard, with a laugh. "But I guess you're a little too small to go navigating around from car to car when the train's moving. What's your father's name? I'll have him called out for in the other cars."

"He's Mr. Richard Bobbsey, of Lakeport," said Flossie, "and my mother and sister and brother are with him. My sister is Nan and my brother is Bert. This is my brother, Freddie."

"Well, now I guess I know the whole family," laughed the guard, the other passengers joining in a smile. "I'll see if I can find your folks for you, though it's queer they haven't been looking for you themselves. You stay here."

The guard started to go through the other cars of the elevated train, and Freddie called after him:

"If you find my father, please tell him to open the box and take out the yellow bug."

"The yellow bug?" repeated the guard in some surprise. "Is your father an animal trainer?"

"Oh, no," said Flossie, seriously. "Freddie

means one of the tin bugs that go around and around and around. And, if you please, I want a green one."

"Say, I wonder what kind of children these are, anyhow," murmured the guard. "Guess they must belong to a theatre or a circus."

"They look nice," said a man sitting near the door.

"Oh, they're all *right,* that's sure. Well, I'll see if I can find their folks for 'em."

Elevated railroad men in New York get used to doing queer things, and seeing strange sights, so it did not cause much excitement when the guard went into the different cars calling for Mr. Bobbsey. He had to come back to his own car once to call out "Forty-second Street," and to open the gates to let passengers off and others on. Then he closed the gates and called out: "Fiftieth Street next." After that he went again into the cars he had not been in before and called for Mr. Bobbsey. But of course that gentleman did not answer, being a station or two behind by this time.

The guard, not being able to find Mr. or Mrs. Bobbsey, or Nan and Bert, came back to

"WHERE ARE YOU YOUNGSTERS GOING?"

The Bobbsey Twins in a Great City. Page 82

where Flossie and Freddie were now rather anxiously waiting.

"Did you find him?" asked the children eagerly.

"No, I'm sorry to say your father isn't on this train. But don't worry. I'll look out for you, and your father is sure to come for you sooner or later."

"Did you find any of the bugs?" asked Freddie.

"That go around and around and around," added Flossie.

"No," said the guard, laughing, "I didn't. What about them?"

Freddie explained what he meant, and asked if the train could not be stopped while he went into the nearest toy store to buy some more of the tin, crawling toys. But the guard said this could not be done.

"I don't just know what to do with you," he said, scratching his head. "If your father thought, he could telephone to any of the stations where our train will stop—this is an express train and does not make many stops after Sixty-sixth Street till the end of the line. He could have the agent there take you off and keep you until he could come. Or, I might take you to One Hundred and Fifty-fifth Street, which is the end of the line, and have the agent there take charge of you. I don't know what to do."

Just then Flossie thought of something:

"Oh, Freddie!" she cried. "We haven't any tickets or any money, unless you have some, and the conductor will put us off!"

"I've got five cents," said Freddie, taking it out of his small pocket.

"That's only enough for a street-car ride, and this is the elevated railroad," replied his blue-eyed sister. "Oh, what shall we do?" And there was just a little tear in each eye as she looked at the guard.

"What's the matter now?" he asked kindly. "Do you want a bug?"

"No—I mean yes, but not now. We haven't any tickets and the conductor——"

"Didn't you drop your tickets in the chopper's box at the station where you got on?"

"No. We ran on ahead," explained Freddie.

"Ho! I see! You were so small that the ticket chopper didn't see you. Well, don't worry—it will be all right. The road won't lose much by carrying you two."

"You could send the bill to my father," said Flossie. "That's what mother says when she goes to buy things at the store."

"That will be all right," the guard said. "I'll see that you're not put off until the proper time comes. And you save your five cents," he added to Freddie, who was holding up the nickel. "You might want to buy some peanuts."

"Oh, that's so—for the monkeys in the park!" cried Freddie. "I forgot we were going to see them!"

By this time some of the other passengers were interested in the children, asking them many questions and learning the story of their coming to New York on a visit.

"They don't seem worried," said one woman. "And they're quite lost in this big city."

"Oh, we've been lost before," said Flossie easily. "Lots of times!"

"In the woods, too," added Freddie. "And

we heard funny noises. But we weren't scared. Were we, Flossie?"

"Nope. We'll just keep on riding now until Daddy comes for us. It's fun, I think."

"And we don't have to pay for it, either," said Freddie, with satisfaction, as he put away his only piece of money. "I'm going to save this for peanuts for the monkeys."

"Will you save some for me?" asked Flossie. "I'm getting hungry."

"Maybe we'll eat these peanuts all ourselves," said Freddie, after thinking about it for a moment. "We can get some for the monkeys later afterward. I'm hungry, too."

"Well, you've got quite a long trip ahead of you," said the guard in whose car they were. "It's quite a ride to One Hundred and Fifty-fifth Street. I'll ask the gateman at the next stop if your father has telephoned about you. Just sit still."

And so Flossie and Freddie, in the elevated express train, were having a long ride all by themselves. They were not frightened now, for they were sure their father or mother would come for them soon, as he had done the day they were spilled out of the ice-boat and were taken in by Uncle Jack.

"I wonder what that nice woodchopper man is doing now?" asked Flossie. "Uncle Jack, I mean."

"I hope his pain is better," said Freddie. "Maybe we could get him work here on the elevated railroad, chopping tickets at the station." When people drop their tickets into the glass boxes at the elevated or subway stations they are "chopped" into fine pieces by the men who pump the handles up and down. "Uncle Jack chops wood," went on Freddie, "and he could easy chop tickets."

So Flossie and Freddie kept on with their long ride, talking and looking out of the train windows.

CHAPTER IX

IN THE STORE

Mr. Bobbsey bought his tickets, put his change in his pocket, and turned to gather his little party together to take them through the gate, past the ticket chopper.

"Why, where are Freddie and Flossie?" he asked.

Mrs. Bobbsey, Nan, Bert, none of them, had seen the little twins rush past the ticket chopper and on to the train. All began to turn here and there excitedly, looking about for the blue-eyed boy and girl.

"Now, now," said Mr. Bobbsey, "don't worry. You, Bert, and your mother and Nan will wait here at the head of the stairs, while I go down to the street and see if the children went down there again. I'll not be gone long. If they are not close at hand, I'll come back to you before making further search. Now, as I said, don't worry. In a city children are always quickly found."

Mr. Bobbsey did as he said, but, of course, saw nothing of Freddie and Flossie, who were now having a very nice ride and a very good time indeed on the elevated express train.

By this time the ticket chopper, the agent who sold tickets, the station porter and several persons who were waiting to take a train, had heard from Nan and Bert what had happened. These people offered all sorts of advice, but Mr. Bobbsey thought it best to listen to that of the ticket agent, who, of course, would know more about the elevated trains than persons who only rode on them two or three times a day.

The ticket chopper had seen the children rush by him and on to the train, but they had gone by so quickly that he had not been able to stop them, and, as there were a good many people on the platform, he did not know to whom they belonged. So he told the ticket seller and Mr. Bobbsey that Flossie and Freddie had taken the last express train that had passed the station.

"It would have been easy enough to stop them if you'd only known it at first," said the ticket seller; "but they've got the start of you now, and after Sixty-sixth Street these express trains make only a few stops before they reach the end of the line. But I can telephone to one of the ticket sellers at one of the uptown stations and have him meet the train and take the children off."

"What will he do with them?" asked Mrs. Bobbsey.

"Oh, he'll keep 'em safe till you folks get there. The trains run pretty close together at this hour of the day. Your husband can get uptown after 'em so quick that they won't have to wait long."

"What shall we do?" asked Bert.

"We will all go on together," answered his father. "I wish we had taken an automobile to go to the hotel, and then this would not have happened. But Flossie and Freddie would have been disappointed if they had not had the first ride in an elevated train. However, I'm sure it will all come out right."

The ticket agent went into his little office to

telephone on ahead, and have Flossie and Freddie taken from the train and held until their parents could claim them. Meanwhile Mr. Bobbsey and the others waited until this was done before getting on the train that was to take them far uptown in New York.

Something was the matter with the telephone in the first station which the ticket seller called up. He could not get the agent there to talk to him over the wire until the train in which Flossie and Freddie were riding, had whizzed on, after making a short stop.

"Well, I'll catch them at the next station where the train stops," the agent said. This time he managed to get in touch with the agent there, but when the latter understood, and ran out to hail the train, it was already in motion and could not be stopped.

"Well, the third time is always lucky," said the ticket seller who had offered to do what he could to help Mr. Bobbsey. "I'll be sure to catch them now."

He talked over the telephone to another agent and this one answered back that the train was just then pulling out of his station.

"But I'll yell at one of the guards," this agent called into the telephone instrument, "and tell him to put the children off at the next stop. I'll do that," and he rushed out to try to call to one of the trainmen.

"That will be One Hundred and Twenty-fifth Street," said the first agent, as he came out of his little office. "That's the best I can do. Your two little children will be put off the train when it makes the stop there, and the ticket agent will look after them until you get there. You can wait for the next express, or you can take a local train here and change to the express at Sixty-sixth Street."

When the next train came along, they got on, eager and anxious to catch up to the missing children. In order not to be bothered with the hand-baggage, Mr. Bobbsey had called a taxicab and had had the chauffeur take it to the hotel were they were to stop, which was an uptown hotel, near enough to Central Park for Flossie and Freddie to walk over to see the monkeys as often as they wished.

Meanwhile the two runaway children—who really did not mean to run away—were in the express train speeding along. After their first surprise at finding themselves alone, they were not frightened, but continued to look out of the windows and to wonder at the many sights they saw.

"Well, we'll be at the end of this run some time," said the guard, who had been talking with Flossie and Freddie.

"What will you do with us then?" the little boy asked.

"Turn you over to the agent, unless we have some other word about you," the trainman answered. "Wait, we're going to stop here, and there may be a message." He hurried out on the platform.

As the train was leaving that station Flossie and Freddie saw the ticket agent run out, waving his hand, and they heard him shout something to their guard. When the latter came into their car again he said to Flossie and Freddie:

"That message was about you two. The agent said two lost children were on this train and that they were to be put off at the next station and left until their father came for them. You're the only lost children I know of."

"And we're not lost so *very* much," said Flossie slowly. "'Cause *we* are here. It's Daddy and the rest who are lost."

"Well, they'll soon be along—coming on the next train," said the guard. "I'll turn you over to the agent at One Hundred and Twenty-fifth Street and you'll be all right."

This was done. The train came to a stop; many passengers got off and a kind woman took Flossie and Freddie in charge and saw that they got inside the elevated station, where the agent, who had been telephoned to, knew about them and was expecting them.

"Now, just sit right down here and be comfortable," the agent said to the Bobbsey twins. "You'll be all right, and your folks will soon come for you. I have to sit in the office and sell tickets."

The kind woman called a good-bye to the children and went away; so Flossie and Freddie were left by themselves in the elevated railroad station at One Hundred and Twenty-fifth Street.

For a while they sat quietly, watching the people come in to buy tickets or get off trains. The agent did not pay much attention to them, being very busy, for it was toward the close of day when the rush was like the morning, greater than at other times.

"Say! What's that?" suddenly asked Flossie, holding up her chubby hand to tell Freddie to stop whistling, which he was trying to do.

"What's what?" he asked, looking at his sister.

"I hear music," went on Flossie.

"So do I!" exclaimed Freddie.

They both listened, and from somewhere outside they heard the sound again.

"It's a hand organ!" cried Flossie.

"No, it's a hand *piano!*" said Freddie. "Hear how jiggily the tune is."

"Well, it's the same thing," Flossie insisted. "I wonder if there's a monkey with it."

"Let's go downstairs and see," proposed Freddie.

Once Flossie or Freddie made up their minds to do a thing it was almost as good as done—that is, if it were not too hard. This time it seemed easy to do. They looked toward the little office in which the ticket seller had shut himself. He was busy selling tickets.

"He'll not see us," whispered Freddie. "Besides, we're coming right back as soon as we see the monkey."

"And we'll give him some peanuts," added Flossie. "You can buy some with your five cents, Freddie. And we won't give them *all* to the monkey. I want some."

"So do I. Come on, we'll go down."

The agent seemed to have forgotten them. At any rate his door was closed and he could not see them. None of the passengers, hurrying in to buy tickets, paid any attention to the Bobbsey twins. So, hand in hand, Flossie and Freddie went out of the station, and down the long stairs to where they could hear the music of the hand piano.

It was being played by an Italian man in the street, almost under the elevated station, and, as Flossie leaned over the stair railing to look down, she cried out:

"Oh, there is a monkey, Freddie! The man has it on a string!"

"That's good. Do you see peanuts anywhere?"

"Yes, there are some at that stand near the bottom of the stairs. Don't lose your five cents!"

"I won't!"

Freddie hurried down with Flossie. He bought a bag of peanuts, and the children hastened across the street to where a little crowd of boys and girls stood in front of the hurdy-gurdy, or hand piano, listening to the music and watching the monkey. This will draw a crowd, even in New York, where there are many more and stranger sights to be seen.

"Oh, isn't he cute!" cried Flossie, tapping her feet on the sidewalk in time to the music.

"He's coming over this way," said Freddie. "I'm going to give him a peanut."

"But don't let him get the whole bag."

"I won't. Here, Jacko! Have a peanut!" and Freddie held out one to the hurdy-gurdy monkey.

The long-tailed animal lost no time in making a grab for it, and soon he was chewing it hungrily. The man grinding out the music shook the cord which was fast to a collar around the monkey's neck. What the street piano man wanted was pennies and five-cent pieces put in the monkey's red cap. Peanuts were good for Jacko, but money was better for his master.

The monkey well knew what the jerks meant on the cord around his neck. They meant that he must scramble around in the crowd and hold out his cap for pennies. The monkey would much rather have eaten peanuts, but even monkeys can not do as they like in this world.

So, with a chattering sound, and with another look at Freddie, who tossed him a peanut, the monkey, catching the dainty in one paw, started to try to collect some money.

But he must have been a hungry little monkey, for, when he looked at Flossie, and saw on her hat what he thought were red cherries, that monkey made up his mind to get some of them if he could. Though the cherries were made of celluloid, they looked very real, and they might have fooled even a boy or a girl, to say nothing of a monkey.

So with a quick bound Jacko—which seems

to be the name of all those long-tailed chaps—was perched on Flossie's shoulder, tearing at her hat with two paws, trying to pull off what he thought were ripe, red cherries.

"Oh! Oh!" screamed Flossie. "Oh, stop!"

"Wait till I get hold of him!" cried Freddie.

"Come away! Come away froma de littlea gal!" yelled the piano Italian. Some in the crowd laughed and others screamed.

The monkey kept pulling and tearing at Flossie's hat until he had pulled it from her head and then, jumping down off her shoulder to the ground, the animal crouched under the piano and began pulling off the red cherries. But one bite told him they were not real, and then, perhaps frightened at what he had done and fearing he would be punished, the monkey tried to run away.

But he was held by the string on his collar, and the Italian, perhaps afraid that he would be made to pay for Flossie's hat, which his monkey had torn to pieces, pulled Jacko to him, perched him on his shoulder and hurried away, wheeling the street piano.

"Oh, Freddie! Freddie! What shall I do?" cried Flossie, as she looked at her sadly torn hat.

"It's a shame," said a woman in the crowd.

"You'll need a new hat, little girl," said another woman.

That gave Freddie an idea. If his sister needed a new hat he was the one to help her get it. He looked up and down the street. Across the way was a large drygoods store, in one of the windows of which were many hats and other things for girls and ladies to wear.

"Come on, Flossie!" cried Freddie, clasping her hand. "I'll take you there."

"Where?" she asked. Tears had come into her eyes when the monkey tore her nice, new hat. But she did not really cry. "Where are you going to take me, Freddie?" she asked.

"Over to that big store; and we'll buy a new hat for you," said the little fellow. "Then we'll go back to the station and wait for Daddy and the rest. Come on. I'll get you a new hat."

Flossie wondered how Freddie was going to do it, but she did not ask. Leaving the torn hat in the street, she went with her brother. He led the way into the big store, which, though it was not one of the large ones of New York, was much bigger than any in Lakeport.

"Well, little ones, what can I do for you?" asked one of the tall men in the store, as Flossie and Freddie strolled in. "Are you with your parents?"

"No, sir, we're all alone," spoke up Freddie. "We were lost on an express train, but we're waiting for my father and mother and Bert and Nan. But a monkey chewed up Flossie's hat and I want a new one for her. You sell hats, don't you?"

CHAPTER X

LOST UNDERGROUND

Flossie and Freddie looked up at the tall man, who smiled kindly down at them. He seemed to be laughing at something, though whether it was Flossie's flaxen hair, now rather tangled because the monkey had pulled off her hat, or because Freddie looked so funny asking his question, the children could not tell.

"So you want a hat for the little girl?" asked the floorwalker, as the man was called. He walked up and down in the store to see that the clerks waited properly on the customers, and he told strangers where to go.

"Flossie wants a hat," went on Freddie. "The monkey ate the cherries off hers."

"No; he didn't really *eat* them," Flossie explained, anxious to have everything just right. "He *tried* to chew 'em, but he didn't like 'em. Anyhow, my hat's gone!"

"What kind of a hat did you want?" asked the store man, not quite sure how to treat the children.

"One with feathers on," suggested Freddie.

"No, I want one with flowers on!" insisted Flossie.

"How much did you want to pay?" asked the man, shaking his head in a puzzled way.

"My father will pay," replied Freddie. "You just send the bill to him—Mr. Richard Bobbsey, of Lakeport. He has a lumber mill and——"

"What seems to be the trouble?" broke in a new voice, and the two children, as well as the floorwalker, turned to see standing near them a stout man, with gray hair, who was smiling kindly at them.

"Oh, Mr. Whipple!" exclaimed the tall man, glad to have some one else to help him. "I don't know what to do about these children. They want a hat for the little girl, and——"

"It's because a monkey ate Flossie's hat!" broke in Freddie. "We're lost. We were on an express train, but we got off and we heard music and please charge it to our father—

charge the hat, I mean, not the music, for we didn't pay anything for that. Did we Flossie?"

"No; but I'm not going to have a hat with feathers on. I want one with flowers on, and I wish mamma was here—or Nan—to help pick it out."

"I'll help you," offered Freddie kindly.

"I guess you had better come with me," said the stout man, who, as the children learned afterward was Mr. Daniel Whipple, owner of the big store into which Flossie and Freddie had wandered. "I'll take you up to my office," Mr. Whipple went on, "and you can tell me about yourselves. I'll try to find your folks for you."

"And can I get a hat?" asked Flossie.

"Yes, I think so," the store owner answered. "Send one of the clerks from the children's hat department to my office with some hats that will do for this little girl," he went on, and the floorwalker said he would.

"We'll be all right now, Flossie," said Freddie, as they followed their new friend. In a little while Flossie was fitted with just the hat she wanted, and Mr. Whipple was listening to the story told in turn by the two children.

"Your father is probably on his way up to get you now," said Mr. Whipple. "He'll expect to find you in the elevated station, but you will not be there. I'll send one of my clerks over to tell the agent you are here, and to send your father over when he comes. But I think I'll keep you two tots here, because——"

"We might get lost again—we get lost lots of times," said Freddie with a smile. "It's nice here. I like it!" and, very much at home, he looked around the office of the store owner.

It was almost closing time, and Mr. Whipple was wondering whether in case the children's father did not come it would not be better to take them to his own home, when the clerk came back from the elevated station with Mr. Bobbsey himself.

"Oh, Daddy!" cried Flossie and Freddie.

"Well, you two certainly gave me a fine chase!" exclaimed Mr. Bobbsey, with a smile, hugging his "little fat fireman" and his "fat fairy," one after the other. "Where in the world have you been?"

"Oh, we heard a hand organ and we went to look at the monkey and it chewed Flossie's hat and we're here!" gasped Freddie, all in one breath.

"And I got a new hat, and you'll please pay for it, Daddy," added Flossie. "And did you bring my bugs—the ones that go around and around and around?" she asked.

"Yes, Flossie, I have them. But what's all this about a hat?"

"I bought her a new one," explained Freddie, "but I didn't have any money to pay for it, so we charged it."

"The little girl seemed to need one, Mr. Bobbsey," said the store owner.

"Oh, that will be all right. I'm glad to pay for it, Mr.—er——"

"Whipple is my name," said the store man. "Daniel Whipple."

"Whipple!" exclaimed Mr. Bobbsey, and a thoughtful look came over his face. "Daniel Whipple," and he seemed to be trying to think of something he had heard a long while before.

"Yes; you may have seen it in my advertisements. I advertise in the papers every day."

"Ah, yes, I presume so," said Mr. Bobbsey. "Thank you very much, Mr. Whipple, for looking after the children for me. I reached the One Hundred and Twenty-fifth Street elevated station a little while ago, and the ticket agent there was very much excited because the children had slipped out while he was in his office.

"We were just trying to think where they could have gone, when your clerk came up to say they were here. Now I'll take them to their mother, who is quite anxious about them."

"I can well believe she is," said Mr. Whipple. "Come and see me again," he invited Flossie and Freddie, who, after their father had paid for the new hat, went away with him.

A little later they were safe in the hotel where the Bobbsey family was to live while in New York. Mrs. Bobbsey, Bert and Nan were already there, and quite glad to see the two runaways, you may be sure.

"What a lot of adventures you must have had!" cried Nan, when Flossie and Freddie had told her a few of the things that had happened.

"We did!" laughed Freddie. "You ought to have seen that monkey's face when he bit on those make-believe cherries on Flossie's hat!" and Freddie laughed loudly.

"Anyhow I got a new hat!"

"That Mr. Whipple was a fine man," said Freddie.

"Indeed he must be," agreed Mrs. Bobbsey, and then, seeing a strange look on her husband's face, she asked:

"What is the matter? Are you worried?"

"No, but I am trying to remember where I have heard that name before. But so much has happened to-day that I can't recall it."

It had been indeed, a full day since the Bobbsey twins had left their home in Lakeport that morning, and Mrs. Bobbsey insisted on Flossie and Freddie, at least, going to bed early. This the small twins were glad enough to do, after they had told Nan and Bert the different things that had happened after they got on the express train.

"It was an awful splendid store," said Flossie, in speaking about Mr. Whipple's establishment.

"Bigger'n any store in Lakeport," added her twin.

"And the nicest clerks that ever was," went on Flossie. "Why, one of 'em had a whole counter full of cologne, and she squirted some on me when I went past, and it smelled awful good!"

After breakfast the next morning, when Mr. Bobbsey had finished sending some telegrams and telephone messages, he asked the children what they first wanted to see in New York.

"The monkeys!" cried Flossie and Freddie.

"I want to go on Fifth avenue and see the lovely shops and stores," said Nan.

"And I want to go to the history museum and see the stuffed animals and the model of a whale," said Bert, who had been reading of this.

"Well, how would you like to go and see some live fish?" asked Mr. Bobbsey. "That ought to satisfy all of you, and Nan can see some stores on the way to the Aquarium. I have to go downtown in New York," he said to his wife, "and I can take the children to the Aquarium at the Battery as well as not."

"All right," said Mrs. Bobbsey. "If you'll do that I'll stay here and rest. Afternoon will do for me to go out. Now mind, Flossie and Freddie, don't get lost again!"

The small twins promised they would not and soon all four were on their way downtown with their father. This time they went in the subway, or underground road, which, as Freddie said, was like one big, long tunnel.

"We'll get out at the Brooklyn Bridge or City Hall Park," said Mr. Bobbsey. "I have to see a man in the City Hall, and from there we can walk to the Battery, as it is a nice day. Or we can ride, if you get too tired."

The children were sure they would not get too tired, and a little later they all got out at the subway station at Brooklyn Bridge.

There were many persons hurrying to and fro, trains coming in and going out, and lights all over, making the children think it was night, though it was in the morning.

"Wait here just a minute," said Mr. Bobbsey, showing the twins a less crowded place where they could stay. "I want to get a magazine over at the news-stand," he added.

The magazine he wanted had been put away under a pile of papers, and as the boy was getting it out Flossie caught sight, down the platform, of a man pasting up on the advertising boards in the underground station, some new posters.

"Oh, maybe it's signs about a circus, Freddie!" cried the little girl. "Come on and watch!"

Freddie was always ready to go, and he had darted off after his sister down the long platform before Bert and Nan saw them. When the two older children missed the younger twins they looked hurriedly about for them.

"There they are—watching that bill-poster," said Bert. For the underground subway stations are much used by advertisers, gaily colored sheets of paper being pasted on boards put there for that purpose.

"You mustn't run away like that!" said Nan to Flossie, as she came up to her sister, to lead her back.

"We wanted to see if it was a circus poster, but it isn't," returned Freddie.

"Well, come on back. Daddy will miss us," declared Bert. He started back—at least he thought he did—for the place where their father had told them to wait for him. But the subway station under the New York sidewalks was so large and rambling, there were so many stairways leading here and there, up and down, and there were so many platforms that it is no wonder Bert went astray.

"Where are you going?" asked Nan at last.

"Well, I was trying to find the place father told us to wait," Bert answered.

"It's over this way," said Nan, pointing just the other direction from the one in which Bert was walking.

"All right, we'll try that, but it seems wrong," he stated.

They walked a little way in that direction. They saw nothing of their father, however, and there were fewer people on the platform where they now were.

"Oh, dear!" cried Flossie, "I'm thirsty! I want a drink!"

"So do I!" added Freddie.

Nan and Bert looked about them. They

were still in the underground station, and they could see trains coming in and going out, and crowds of people hurrying to and fro. But they could not see their father nor the place where he had told them to wait. At last Nan said:

"Bert, I don't know where we are! We're lost!"

CHAPTER XI

FREDDIE AND THE TURTLE

BERT BOBBSEY looked all around the big underground subway station before he answered Nan. Then he took off his cap to scratch his head, as he often did while thinking. Next he looked down at Flossie and Freddie.

If he thought he was going to find the two little twins in a fright at what Nan had said about being lost, Bert was mistaken. The two flaxen-haired tots were looking down the long platform, into the gloom of the long tunnel of the subway.

"Aren't they funny, Freddie?" asked Flossie.

"Yep, awfully funny," was Freddie's answer.

"What's funny?" asked Bert, wishing he could see something at which to laugh.

"Those red and green lights down the track," explained Freddie. "They blink so funny and come up and go out——"

"Just like winking at you," said Flossie. "I like it down here. It isn't like the dark tunnels we went in on the steam cars."

"Well, I'm glad *somebody* likes it," said Bert to Nan. "But say, how do we get out of here?"

"I'm sure I don't know," she said. "When I ran after Flossie I didn't look which way I was going."

"I didn't, either. Queer how we could get lost in a place like this," and Bert seemed worried and spoke more loudly than he intended. Freddie heard what his brother said and looked up quickly.

"Are we *really* lost?" he asked.

"It seems so," answered Nan. "I ran after you two, and we have walked about so many platforms and up and down so many stairs that I can't see or remember the place where Father told us to wait for him."

"Well, there's no danger, that's sure," said Bert. "It's a queer place to be lost in—a subway station. I was never in one before, but if we stay here long enough Dad is sure to find us. Here comes somebody now, looking for us, I guess."

A man in a blue suit, carrying a red lantern, and with white numbers on either side of his cap, walked toward the four twins.

"Is your name Bobbsey?" he asked.

"Yes; but how did you know?" was Bert's question.

"Your father sent me to look for you. He guessed you must have wandered away, and he thought it best to stay where he told you to wait, and let one of us find you. A lot of men are hunting up and down the different platforms for you."

"Well, I'm glad you found us!" sighed Nan. "We didn't know what to do."

"Just come with me," said the subway guard. "I'll take you to your father," and he did, leading the children down a long platform and over a sort of bridge, then down a flight of steps. Though they did not know it, the twins had wandered quite a distance from the place Mr. Bobbsey had left them.

The subway station was a rambling place, with several doors to go in by and come out of, a number of platforms and stairways, and wiser persons than four small children could easily become confused there.

When Mr. Bobbsey came back, after buying his magazine, and could not find his children, he guessed what had happened, and wisely asked a guard to make a search, instead of doing it himself.

"For I don't come to New York often enough to be sure of finding my way around in all the odd nooks and corners," said the lumber merchant.

"And it wasn't a circus poster at all!" said Freddie, after Flossie had told what had caused her to wander away. "It was only about chewing gum."

Speaking of chewing gum made Flossie remember she was thirsty, and after Mr. Bobbsey had thanked the man with the red lantern, and had explained to Freddie that it was used to stop trains in case of an accident, the Bobbsey party went up out of the underground station and into a candy store.

"I know what I'm going to have!" exclaimed Freddie.

"So do I!" cried Flossie.

"Chocolate soda!"

"Yes! And I want plenty of cream on top!"

"Suppose they haven't got any chocolate soda?" remarked Mr. Bobbsey, with a twinkle in his eye.

"Oh, I know they've got chocolate soda," remonstrated his little son. "They always have chocolate soda at soda fountains! Don't they, Flossie?"

"Of course they do! I don't think it would be a real soda fountain if they didn't have chocolate soda," replied the little girl.

"I think I'm going to have an orange phosphate," said Bert.

"And that is just what I am going to have too," added Nan.

"Phosphate!" cried Freddie in wonder. "I wouldn't drink any phosphate! That's what they make matches of."

"Oh, just hear that!" cried Bert, laughing. "Freddie thinks they make matches of phosphate."

"They do, too!" answered the little boy.

"You are thinking of phosphorus, Freddie," explained Mr. Bobbsey. "That is different, and it is poisonous." Then the drinks were ordered and quickly served.

"And now I want to go to see the big fish!" said Freddie, sipping the last drops of his sweet drink. "Are there any animals in the 'quarium, Daddy?"

"Well, there aren't any lions or tigers," answered Mr. Bobbsey. "We'll go to see them later in Bronx Park. But, of course, fish are animals. It won't take me long to run into City Hall and see my friend. Then we'll go to the Aquarium."

Left on the top steps of the City Hall building, this time the Bobbsey twins were found safely there when their father came out, and a little later they were on their way to Battery Park in a Broadway street car, that ran on the ground.

"We've ridden under the ground in the subway, over the ground in the elevated and now we're riding *on* the ground," said Nan. "New York is a funny place!"

The Aquarium, as those of you know who have seen it, is in the round, brown stone building, on a point of land almost the very end of the island of Manhattan. It is where the North and East rivers come together to form New York Bay, and, years ago, this building was where the immigrants, or people who came to the United States from other countries, were kept for a while until they could be sent out West, or down South, or wherever they wanted to go.

Now it is a place where many fish, big, little, ugly and beautiful, are shown in tanks of water so the boys and girls can see what strange things are in the ocean, rivers and lakes of this world.

Led by Mr. Bobbsey, Bert and Nan, with Flossie and Freddie trailing on behind, walked around the big building, looking in the glass tanks wherein swam the fish.

"What's over there?" asked Freddie, pointing to where a crowd of people were standing near some pools in the middle of the floor.

"Oh, different big fish—a sea lion, alligators and turtles," said Mr. Bobbsey.

"Let's look at the sea lion!" called Flossie.

"I want to see a swimming turtle," said Freddie. "I had a mud turtle once, but he went away."

"You shall see everything," promised Mr. Bobbsey.

They went over to the pool, where a number of large alligators, and one crocodile, were lying in or out of the water. Some were lazily swimming about, and the crocodile was asleep out on the stone ledge, with his big mouth wide open.

"He's waiting for some one to come along and feed him," said Bert.

"I guess he'd eat a lot," laughed Freddie, looking at the rows of big teeth in the crocodile's mouth.

They passed on to the pool of the sea lion. That sleek, brown animal was swimming about like a big fish, now and then stopping under one of the pipes where the water ran into his pool, and holding his mouth under the little stream as though taking a drink. Now and then he barked like a dog.

Around the stone ledge, or wall of the pool,

was a wire grating, and near the floor was a sort of pipe running all around, so the smaller children could step up on this to look in—something which the big folk did not have to do.

"Be careful!" cried Nan, as Flossie leaned well over the edge to get a better look at the sea lion. "You might fall in."

"She could get a ride on his back if she did," said Freddie.

"Well, I'm not going to!" exclaimed Flossie, drawing back, a little frightened, as the seal splashed the water right under her, some drops going in her face.

They watched the seal for a while, went over to the other tanks, where some sturgeon and other big fish swam about, and then Freddie called:

"I want to see the big turtles! Where are they?"

"Over here," said Mr. Bobbsey, leading the way toward the south end of the building near the tank, where the green moray—a sort of big eel—was lying half in and half out of a piece of sewer pipe put in his tank to make him feel more at home. "There are the big turtles," and Mr. Bobbsey lifted Flossie up over the rail so she could look down more easily.

There were some very large turtles in the tank, swimming by moving their broad flippers. Sometimes they would swim about close to the white tiled bottom of the tank, but the water was clear, so they could be seen easily. Again the turtles would rise to the top, so that their big, hard shells were out of water, like a raft which the boys build to play with when the city's vacant lots or country meadows are flooded in the Spring.

In one end of the tank was a big turtle—the largest of all—swimming by himself, and overhead, hung by a wire from the room, was a stuffed one, larger yet. This, so a sign near it said, was a "leather-back turtle," and when alive had weighed eight hundred and fifty pounds.

"Whew!" whistled Bert, looking at the big, stuffed fellow. "He could swim around with two or three boys on *his* back."

"I'd like to have had a ride on him," cried

Freddie. "But this one is pretty big, too!" and he pointed down at the large swimming turtle, which, just then, stuck his head up out of the water. He seemed to be nearly a yard long and almost as broad.

"Oh!" screamed Flossie, as she saw the big turtle so close to her. "Can he get out of the water, Daddy?"

"No, indeed," laughed Mr. Bobbsey.

"I can't see him very good," said Freddie, and he gave a little jump up from the foot-rail on which he was standing.

Freddie must have jumped up harder and farther than he had any idea of, for before Bert, who was standing near his little brother, could put out a hand to hold him, the flaxen-haired twin had fairly dived over the rail, and down into the tank he fell with a great splash.

No, not such a great splash, either, for Freddie did not fall directly into the water. Instead, only his two fat legs and feet went in, for the small boy landed, sitting right up on the broad back of the big turtle! Right down on the turtle's back fell Freddie Bobbsey!

CHAPTER XII

IN THE THEATRE

There was a scream from Nan, another from Flossie, and a sort of grunt of surprise from Bert, as they saw Freddie disappear over the railing of the tank, and come into view a second later on the back of the turtle, which was as much surprised as, probably, the little boy himself.

"Here, Freddie! What are you doing down there?" asked Mr. Bobbsey, before he thought what he was saying. He and his wife had so often to ask what Flossie or Freddie were doing, as the smaller twins were so often in mischief, that the father did it this time.

"Oh, the turtle will eat him up! The turtle will eat Freddie up!" cried Flossie.

Freddie, too, after the first shock of surprise, was frightened, and as he clung with both hands to the edges of the turtle's shell he looked over his shoulder, toward his father and the others, and cried:

"Oh, get me out, Daddy! Get me out!"

The cries of the children, and the call of Mr. Bobbsey, had drawn a crowd around the turtle pool, and among the throng were some of the attendants on duty in the Aquarium.

"What's the matter?" asked one, elbowing his way through the crowd to the side of Mr. Bobbsey, who was trying to climb over the rail to go to the rescue of his little boy.

"Freddie fell in," explained Bert. "He's on the back of the big turtle!"

"Good land!" cried the man. "What will happen here next? Come back, sir," he went on to Mr. Bobbsey, "I'll get him out for you."

"Then please be quick. He may fall off and the turtle may bite him or drown him," said Freddie's father.

"Well, the turtle *could* give him a bad bite," returned the Aquarium man. "But if he holds on a little longer I'll get your boy."

The man jumped up on the ledge of the pool and made his way to the piece of wood that held up the heavy wire screen which divided the turtle pool into two parts, keeping the one big turtle away from the others. All this while Freddie sat on the shell of the big turtle, his chubby legs dangling in the water, and his hands grasping the edges of the shell behind the front flippers. The turtle's neck was so short that it could not turn its head to bite Freddie, nor could the big flippers reach him. As they had no claws on the ends, they would have done no harm, anyhow, if they had brushed him.

The greatest danger was that the turtle might suddenly sink down to the bottom of the pool, and, though it was not very deep, it was deep enough to have let Freddie drown.

Even though the small boy could swim, the turtle might attack him, or knock his head under water, which would have been a great danger to Flossie's brother. But, so far, the turtle did not show any wish to sink below the water. It was frightened, that was certain, for it splashed about in the pool and swam as fast as it could, carrying Freddie with it. Freddie was such a small chap, and the turtle was so large, that it did not mind the weight on its back. But there was no telling when it would sink down.

"Take me off! Take me off!" cried Freddie again.

"That's all right," said the Aquarium man. "Don't be afraid, little boy. The turtle won't hurt you, and we'll soon have you off his back. He won't bite you, and you're having a fine ride!"

Freddie, it seemed, had not thought of that before.

"That's so!" he exclaimed, and his face did not show much fright now. "I am having a ride, ain't I?"

Flossie heard this, and then, instead of being afraid her brother would be hurt, she cried out:

"Oh, I want a turtle ride, too!"

"No!" exclaimed Mr. Bobbsey, who was not so worried, now that he saw the Aquarium man on his way to get Freddie. "One turtle ride is enough for the family. Hold fast, Freddie!" he called, as the turtle came around on the side of the pool near to where the Bobbseys stood.

By this time the man was out on the middle of the wooden piece that held the heavy wire netting, and as the turtle swam near that the man leaned over and quickly lifted Freddie from the swimming creature's back.

"There you are, my boy!" cried the man, as he held Freddie out to another attendant who had come to help. "Now you're all right except for wet feet, and we can dry them for you in the engine room.

"We have to keep the boilers going in Winter to warm the water for the tropical fish," said the man to Mr. Bobbsey. "Take your little boy there and we'll dry his shoes and stockings."

"Thank you," said Mr. Bobbsey. By this time Freddie was safely out of the turtle pool, and the big creature, relieved of that strange thing on his back, had sunk down to the bottom of the pool, as though to hide away. It was lucky he had kept himself afloat as long as he had, or Freddie might have been wet all over.

"Well, you do seem to have the queerest things happen to you, Freddie," said his father with a smile. "What will you do next?"

"I—I couldn't help this, Daddy," said the little fellow. "I—I just slipped!"

"Well, don't do it again," said the Aquarium man, with a smile. "If you had fallen in the other pool, where there are half a dozen turtles, though none as large as the one you rode on, you might have been bitten. But you're all right. Now come along and we'll dry you out."

It was an easy matter to dry Freddie's feet and legs in front of the warm furnaces in the boiler room, but his shoes and stockings did not get rid of their wetness so soon. And, as Mr. Bobbsey did not want to wait, he sent one of the attendants out to buy new shoes and stockings for his son. With these on, and carrying the damp ones in a bundle, Freddie was soon ready to go home.

"I guess I've had enough of the 'quarium," he said. "Anyhow I had a funny ride."

"I should say you did!" agreed Bert. "I wish we had a picture of you riding around on the back of that turtle."

Mrs. Bobbsey was at first alarmed, and then she laughed, when told of what had happened.

"FREDDIE FELL IN!" "HE'S ON THE BACK OF A BIG TURTLE."

The Bobbsey Twins in a Great City. *Page* 128

She made Freddie drink some hot milk, so he would not get cold, but he told her the water of the turtle pool was warm, as it always is in Winter, and he said: "I don't think I'll even have the snuffles," which he did not, as the next day proved.

For two or three days Mr. Bobbsey was busy attending to his business in New York, but he found time to take the children to see the many sights.

"I want to go on a ferryboat and across the Brooklyn Bridge," said Flossie, one day.

"Oh, I want to go on a ferryboat too. And I want to see what makes the ferryboat go!" cried Freddie eagerly.

"All right; I'll take you out to-day," answered Mr. Bobbsey. "And I'll show you as much of the ferryboat as I can," he added.

Then they went across the Brooklyn Bridge on a car, and later on they took quite a trip on the ferryboat to St. George, Staten Island, and back, and Freddy even got a glimpse into the engine-room of the boat and went home satisfied.

"There is so much to see!" exclaimed Nan,

after a day spent in the Bronx Park, where there are many animals. "I don't believe we could see it *all* in a year."

"That's right," agreed Bert. "But we're going to see something good this afternoon."

"What?" asked Flossie. "Are we going to another 'quarium?"

"No, to a matinée in the theatre," said her larger brother. "It's an awful funny play—anyhow, the billboard pictures are."

"Are we all going?" asked Freddie.

"Yes," answered Mrs. Bobbsey. "We are all going."

Much excited over the joys before them, for in Lakeport there was only one theatre, and plays did not show there often, the Bobbsey twins made ready to go to the matinée. Flossie and Nan wore new frocks, and Bert and Freddie had new suits, so they were quite dressed-up, they felt.

The play was a very amusing one, and the children laughed so hard that Freddie at last rolled off his seat and had to be picked up by his father.

But this only made ali the more fun, and

the people around the Bobbsey family joined in the laughter when an usher helped Mr. Bobbsey place Freddie in his proper place again.

Then the curtain went down on the first act, and as the lights were turned up the children looked about them. Freddie found himself seated next to a boy about his own age, who, with an elderly lady, had come in after the performance began. This was why Freddie had not noticed his little neighbor before.

"Isn't this a dandy show!" cried Freddie.

"The best I ever saw," answered the boy. "What's your name?"

"Freddie Bobbsey. What's yours?"

"Laddie Dickerson. Where do you live?"

"We live away up in Lakeport, but we're staying at the Parkview Hotel."

"Why—why, that's where *we* live, my mother and my uncle and my aunt. My father is dead. We live at the hotel, except in the Summer, when we go to the seashore. What floor are you on?"

"The tenth. I know 'cause I holler it out when we come up in the elevator."

"Why, *we* live on the tenth floor, too," said

Laddie Dickerson. "It's funny I never saw you."

"And it's funny I never saw you," replied Freddie. "Say, come and play with me, will you?"

"Sure I will! We'll have lots of fun. I've got a train of cars."

"I've got a fire engine!" said Freddie, his eyes big with delight. "Oh, what fun we'll have!"

"Hush, Freddie dear," said his mother, for the little boy was talking rather loudly. "The curtain is going up again."

CHAPTER XIII

THE "RESCUE" OF FREDDIE

DURING the rest of the play the attention of Freddie and Flossie, who sat near him, was divided between Laddie, the new boy, and the things happening on the stage. Both were so jolly—the funny things the actors did and the chance of having a new playmate—that the two smaller Bobbsey twins did not know which was best.

"Don't you like this show?" asked Freddie of Laddie, when the curtain went down again.

"Yes. It's great! But I'm glad you're comin' to play with me," Laddie answered.

"So'm I," answered Freddie. "You're glad too, aren't you, Flossie?"

"Of course I am," said the little girl.

"Does *she—she* play with you?" asked Laddie, nodding his head toward Freddie's little sister, as if in surprise.

"Of course she does. We have lots of fun. Why?"

"But she's a *girl!*"

"Of *course* she's a girl," agreed Freddie. "She couldn't be my sister if she wasn't a *girl.* I've got another sister, too, but she's bigger. She's sitting on the end of the row. She plays with Bert and Flossie plays with me. We're two sets of twins. Don't you like girls?"

"Well, I don't know," said Laddie slowly. "I never played with 'em much. I—I like your sister, though. She can play with us. Do you ever play store?"

"Lots of times," said Freddie. "We take some dirt for sugar, some little stones for eggs, some big stones for loaves of bread, clam shells and pieces of tin for dishes—we have lots of fun like that. But we haven't had any fun that way since we came to New York. I fell on a turtle's back in the 'quarium, though, and had a ride."

"You did!" cried Laddie, so loudly that many persons in near-by seats turned to smile at him.

"Sure I did," answered Freddie. "I'll tell

you about it. I was scared at first, but——"

"Laddie, dear, the curtain is going up and you had better keep quiet," said the elderly lady who was with the new boy.

"Is she your mother?" Freddie asked.

"No, she's my aunt. My mother is out in California, but she's comin' home soon, and I'm glad of it, though my aunt is awful nice."

"Hush!" exclaimed Mrs. Bobbsey, thinking it was Freddie talking, for now the last act had started. So the two little boys quieted down, each one resolved to start talking again as soon as he could.

The last act of the show proved to be uproariously funny, and Freddie laughed and laughed until he was in danger of rolling on the floor again. But he was held fast in his seat, and so that danger was averted.

"Say, Freddie, wouldn't you like to be an actor man?" questioned Flossie, during a brief interval in the play.

"Sure, I'm going to be an actor man when I grow up," responded her brother quickly.

"But you're going to be a fireman too, ain't you?" queried his sister.

"Of course! I'm going to be an actor man and a fireman too," replied Freddie. "I can act in a theatre when there aren't any fires to be put out."

"But what would you do if you were all dressed up as an actor man when you had to go out to put out a fire?" asked his sister.

"Oh, I'd just tell the people that I couldn't act any more, and then I'd run right out and get my engine," answered Freddie simply.

"I guess I'd like to be an actor man too," put in Laddie. "I heard a big boy tell once that they earn bushels and bushels of money."

"Sure, they do," answered Freddie. "They make a thousand dollars a minute, I guess."

The play ended in a jolly lot of fun and music, and everybody was laughing when the final curtain went down. Fathers and mothers, who had come to bring their children, talked with one another, though they were strangers, and it was because of this that Mrs. Bobbsey, when Freddie and Laddie started to talk together again about the turtle ride, nodded and smiled at the elderly lady with whom Laddie had come to the theatre.

"My little boy seems to have taken quite a fancy to yours," said the twins' mother.

"Oh, he isn't my boy, though I love him as though he were," said this lady. "Laddie is my sister-in-law's boy, but she is in California. My husband and I are taking care of Laddie."

"And Freddie is coming to play store and steam cars and automobile and steam engine, with me, and—and——"

Laddie paused, trying to think of something else.

"Fireman," said Freddie. "We're going to play fireman."

"Oh, yes," agreed Laddie. "I forgot about that. We're going to play fireman."

"And I'm going to play with 'em," added Flossie.

"Yes, she can come," said Laddie to his aunt. "I guess I'll like her, though I don't know much about playin' with girls," he added.

"Well, you seem to have it all settled," laughed his aunt. The Bobbseys and their new friends were standing in the theatre aisle, waiting for the crowds ahead of them to pass out.

"We're strangers in New York," added Mrs.

Bobbsey. "We are staying at the Parkview Hotel——"

"Why, that's where my husband and I have been living for a number of years," said Freddie's aunt. "My husband has a department store in Harlem, but he likes to live in this section. I like the hotel very much. Won't you let me call to see you?"

Mrs. Bobbsey said she would be very glad to, and so the two ladies, having thus met, became friends, which Laddie and Freddie had done a little while before. Laddie's aunt, whose name was Mrs. Whipple, said she would be glad to have Freddie and Flossie, as well as Nan and Bert, come in to play with Laddie.

"Though I am afraid your two larger twins are rather old for our small boy," said Mrs. Whipple, who had no children of her own.

"Yes, Nan and Bert are getting a little older," said Mrs. Bobbsey. "But Freddie and Flossie will be delighted to have a new playfellow."

So it was arranged that the next day the two small twins were to go to the Whipple apartment to play with Laddie, and Flossie and Freddie could hardly wait for that time to come.

"Oh, I think New York is just the *nicest* place!" said Flossie, as she talked with Freddie about whether or not she might bring one doll with her when she went to Laddie's hotel home.

"It's dandy!" said Freddie. "Don't you wish you were coming with us, Bert?"

"Pooh! Dad is going to take *me* to see the airships go up down at Governor's Island. They go up even in Winter, for the airmen want to get used to the cold, I guess," Bert said.

"Oh, I want to see the airships!" cried Freddie. "Can't Daddy take me, too?" he asked his mother.

"Well, not this time, Freddie," said Mr. Bobbsey. "You and Flossie are going to have some fun with Laddie. I'll take you later."

And with this the small twins had to be satisfied. So, while Nan and Bert were taken downtown, to get a glimpse of the airships flying over New York bay, which the bird-like craft did, in charge of army officers, who wished to learn to fly, even when there was snow on the ground, the small twins, taking some of their toys with them, went to the hotel rooms where Laddie Dickerson lived with his aunt.

"Did you bring the bugs that go around and around and around?" asked Flossie, as their mother knocked at Mrs. Whipple's door.

"Yep," answered Freddie. "And I brought my toy fire engine, too. I wonder if she'll let us squirt real water?" and he nodded toward the door that was not yet opened by Laddie's aunt.

"You mustn't do that unless you are told you may," said Mrs. Bobbsey. "If you squirt water you may spoil the wall paper."

"We'll be careful," promised Freddie, and then Mrs. Whipple's maid opened the door, and the twins went in to have a good time.

Laddie was very glad to see them, and he was much amused at the "go-around" bugs. He had a number of toys of his own, and when the children were tired of playing with them, and with those the Bobbsey twins had brought, they began to have a make-believe store.

"I've got some real store boxes and things," said Laddie, as he brought them out from his play-room.

"Oh, they *are* real!" cried Flossie, as she saw them. "Isn't they grand! Where'd you get 'em?"

"My Uncle Dan gave them to me," said Laddie. "He keeps a real store, and he sells hats and dresses and lots of things."

"What's the name of his store?" asked Freddie.

"He's Daniel Whipple," answered Laddie. "He is my mother's brother—her name was Whipple, too, before she was married to my father. And my middle name is Whipple. I go to my Uncle Dan's store lots of times; it's an awful big one."

"I know it is!" cried Freddie. "I've been in it!"

"You have?" cried Laddie in surprise.

"When?" asked Flossie. "When were we in Laddie's uncle's store?"

"Don't you 'member?" went on Freddie. "It was the time the monkey chewed your hat, Flossie. We went into a store to buy a new one, and Daddy came there and found us and the man's name was Whipple."

"That's right—it was," agreed Flossie. "Oh, isn't that *funny!* And now we're playing with *you,* Laddie."

"It is queer. I'm going to tell my aunt."

And when Laddie did, Mrs. Whipple remembered having heard her husband tell about the two little lost children who came into his department store after a street-piano monkey had spoiled a little girl's hat.

"And to think *you* two are those same children!" cried Mrs. Whipple. "It is quite remarkable, and New York such a big place as it is. I must tell my husband. He's Laddie's uncle, you know."

"I've got another uncle, too, but we don't know where he is," went on Laddie.

"Is he lost at sea?" asked Freddie. "If he is, I know how to find him. Just ask Tommy Todd's father. He was shipwrecked, and me and Flossie found him in a snow storm."

"You must tell me about that some time," said Mrs. Whipple. "But Laddie's other uncle isn't lost at sea, so far as we know. It's too sad a story to tell to children. But Mr. Whipple has a brother, who is also a brother to Laddie's mother, but this brother has long been lost."

"How'd he get lost?" asked Freddie. "Did he go to the store and couldn't find his way back?"

"No, my child. It was different from that. I'll tell you, perhaps, another time. Go on with your play now."

So Laddie, Freddie and Flossie went back to their "store," and had lots of fun. Then they played other games, using Freddie's fire engine and Laddie's train of cars, and even Flossie's doll, who rode as a passenger.

"Well, what'll we do next?" asked Freddie, when he and Laddie had taken turns squirting water from the fire engine in the bath room.

"Let's play automobile," said Laddie. "I can get——"

He stopped talking and seemed to be listening.

"What's the matter?" asked Flossie, as Laddie hurried to a window that looked down into a side street.

"It's a fire!" cried Laddie. "I can hear the puffers! Come on! It's right down this side street!"

Flossie and Freddie looked out of the window long enough to see a crowd of people in front of a store not far from the hotel, which was on a corner. And in the street, which was a side one, as Laddie had said, were a number of fire engines.

"Let's go down!" cried Freddie, all excited at what he saw.

"Oh, you mustn't!" gasped Flossie.

"Course we can," declared Laddie. "My aunt always lets me look at a fire when it's near here, and this is awful close. Maybe this hotel will burn down."

"Oh-o-o-o!" cried Flossie. "Where's my doll?" And she ran to get her pet.

"Come on, we'll go!" said Freddie to Laddie. "Girls don't like fires, but we boys do."

"Sure," said Laddie. "We'll go, all right. My aunt's looking out the front window, and we can go out the side door and down the elevator," he went on. "I know all the elevator men, 'cause I've lived in this hotel a whole year. My aunt won't care 'cause she won't see us, so she won't be worried. I don't like her to worry."

"Me either," said Freddie. So the two little boys, making sure Mrs. Whipple was still looking from the front windows of her apartment, to see what all the excitement was about, stole out of a door into the side hall and so reached the elevators.

"Down, George!" called Laddie to the colored elevator man.

"Down it am, Master Laddie," was the good-natured answer. "Where is yo'all gwine?"

"To see the fire," was the answer. "Don't he talk funny?" asked Laddie of Freddie, as they left the elevator at the ground floor.

"He talks just like our colored cook, Dinah," said Freddie. "Did you ever see her?"

"Nope."

"You ought to eat some of her pancakes," went on Freddie. "I'll write, when I have a chance, and ask her to send you some."

"Oh, hear the engines whistlin'!" cried Laddie. "Hurry up, or maybe they'll be gone before we get there."

The fire was not near enough to the hotel to cause any danger, though many of the hotel guests were excited, and so no attention was paid to the small boys, Freddie and Laddie, as they hurried out to see all that was going on. There was a crowd in the side street and more engines and hook and ladder trucks were dashing up to help put out the fire.

From the blazing store great clouds of black smoke were pouring out, and firemen were rushing here and there. Laddie looked for a while at the exciting scene and then he called to Freddie:

"I'm going back and get my aunt. She likes to look at fires."

"All right; I'll wait for you here," Freddie said. They had been standing not far away from the side entrance to the hotel, and as Laddie turned to go back after his aunt, Freddie walked down the street a little way, nearer the fire.

"I can see Laddie and his aunt when they come," thought the small boy.

But just then a bigger crowd, anxious to watch the fire, came around the corner, and, rushing down the narrow side street, fairly pushed Freddie ahead of them.

"Here! Wait a minute! I don't want to go so fast!" cried the little fellow. "I want to wait for Laddie!"

No one paid any attention to him, and he was swept along, half carried off his feet by the rush, until at last he found himself standing alone, almost in front of the burning store.

"Oh, I can see fine here!" thought Freddie. "I wish Laddie and his aunt would hurry and come here. Wow! This is great!"

Freddie was so excited watching the puffing engines, seeing the big black clouds of smoke, and the leaping, darting tongues of fire from the windows of the burning building, also watching the firemen squirt big streams of water on the blaze, that he did not think of himself, and the first he realized was when some one shouted at him:

"Stand back there, youngster!"

Freddie did not know he was the "youngster" meant, and stood where he was.

"Get back there!" cried the voice again. "You may be hurt!"

But Freddie was busy watching the fire. He wished he had brought his own little engine with him.

"I could squirt water on some of the little sparks, anyhow," he said to himself. "I guess I'll go back and get it, and find Laddie and his aunt."

Freddie was about to turn when suddenly he saw a fireman in a white rubber coat, which showed he was one of the chiefs, or head men, rushing toward him.

"Get back! Get back!" cried this fireman. "Don't you know you're inside the fire lines!"

Then for the first time Freddie noticed that back of him was stretched a rope, behind which stood the crowd of men and boys. Freddie was so small that he had slipped under the rope, not knowing it. He had either slipped under himself or been pushed by the throng.

"Get back! Get back!" cried the fireman.

The next instant there was a loud noise, as if a gun had been fired, and Freddie felt himself being lifted up and carried along quickly.

CHAPTER XIV

THE STORE CAMP

THE noise like a gun which Freddie heard was made when something exploded, or blew up, in the burning store, and at first Freddie thought he had been blown up with it and was flying through the air.

Then, as he opened his eyes (for he had closed them when the strange thing began to happen) he saw that he was in the arms of the fireman with the white rubber coat, and the fireman was smiling down at him.

"Am I—am I hurted?" Freddie asked.

"Bless your little heart! Of course not!" was the answer. "But you might have been if you had stayed where you were—not so much hurt by the fire, for that's almost out—as by the crowd. How did you get past the fire lines?"

"I—I didn't see 'em," said Freddie. "Back

in Lakeport, where I live, we don't have fire lines, though I've got a fish line."

"Humph! You're from the country, all right. Where do you live, and how comes it your father let you out in the streets during a fire?"

"I live in the Parkview Hotel and my father didn't let me out. He's gone to see the air-ships with Nan and Bert, and Laddie and I came out to see the fire ourselves. Flossie stayed with her doll. Laddie went back to get his aunt, 'cause she likes fires—I mean to see 'em—and I waited for him, and—and——"

"Yes, I guess you don't know *what* happened next," laughed the fireman. "But as I want to telephone to headquarters about one of the engines that is broken, I'll use the hotel 'phone, and, at the same time, take you back where you belong. You're too little to get inside the ropes at a New York fire."

"I'm going to be a fireman when I grow up," said Freddie, as the assistant chief carried him into the corridor of the hotel.

"Well, that won't be for some time yet, and while you're waiting to grow up don't go too near fires—they're dangerous. There you are, and I think some one is looking for you," the fireman went on, as he saw a lady rushing toward him when he set Freddie down.

"That's my mother," said Freddie.

"Oh, Freddie! Where have you been?" cried Mrs. Bobbsey, for when she heard of a fire she went in search of the two small twins, and could not find them in Mrs. Whipple's rooms.

"I've been to the fire, and I was rescued," answered Freddie. "He did it," and he pointed to the white-coated fireman.

"Oh, he really wasn't in any real danger," the assistant chief said, taking off his heavy helmet and bowing to Mrs. Bobbsey. "He was inside the fire lines and I carried him here."

"Oh, I can't thank you enough!" cried Freddie's mother. "I never knew him to do such a thing as that before. But he is simply wild about fires!"

"Yes, most boys are."

Then the fireman telephoned about the broken engine. Freddie told his mother how he and Laddie came to go down to watch the "puffers" (part of which story Flossie had already told Mrs. Bobbsey), and then along came Laddie and his aunt. Mrs. Whipple was almost as much worried as was Mrs. Bobbsey.

But everything came out all right; no one was hurt, and the fire, though it badly burned the store in which it started, did not get near the hotel or any other buildings.

But Freddie could not forget about his "rescue," as he called it, and when his father, with Nan and Bert, came home that evening the story had all to be told over again.

"But you and Laddie did wrong to go down to the fire without telling Laddie's aunt," said Mr. Bobbsey to his small son. "You must never do it again!"

"I never will," promised Freddie. "But I was rescued all right, wasn't I?"

"I guess so," and Mr. Bobbsey had to turn his head away so Freddie would not see his smile.

Laddie, Flossie and Freddie soon became fast friends, and when the smaller Bobbsey twins were not being taken about New York, to see what to them were very wonderful sights, they were either playing in the rooms of Mrs. Whipple or in their own at the hotel.

Bert and Nan were a little too old for this kind of fun, but they met, in the same hotel, a brother and sister of about their own age—Frank and Helen Porter—with whom they had good times.

Mr. Bobbsey had to spend many days looking after the business that had brought him to New York, but Mrs. Bobbsey was free to go about with the children. She took Nan and Bert shopping with her sometimes, leaving Flossie and Freddie with Mrs. Whipple. This suited the small twins, for Laddie and they were great friends and played well together.

Other times Bert and Nan would go to the park, or somewhere with the Porter brother and sister, and Mrs. Bobbsey would take Flossie and Freddie to a matinée or the moving pictures.

"Oh, I think New York is just the nicest place in the world," said Nan one afternoon, after a trip she and Bert had had on top of a

Fifth avenue automobile stage, Frank and Helen Porter having gone with them.

"Yes, it is nice," agreed Bert. "But it's nice in Lakeport, too. You can't have fun riding down hill here, and the skating isn't as good as on our Lake Metoka. And I haven't seen an ice-boat since we came here, except in moving pictures. I wonder how Tommy Todd is making out with mine."

"Hasn't he written to you?" asked Nan.

"No; but he promised he would. Guess I'll write him a postal now and ask him how the *Bird* is sailing."

"And I'll write to some of the girls in Lakeport," said Nan.

I had forgotten to tell you that some time before this, Mr. Whipple, the man who owned the store where Flossie's hat was bought the day the monkey chewed up hers, had met the two smaller twins in his wife's rooms one day, when Flossie and Freddie had come to play with Laddie.

"Why, those are the two little children who were on the elevated express," said the store owner, in surprise.

"That's so, you do know them, don't you?" returned Mrs. Whipple.

"I should say I did!" cried her husband, and he told all that had happened, while Mrs. Whipple related how Laddie, Flossie and Freddie had come to know one another in the theatre.

Mr. Whipple, at another time, once more met Mr. Bobbsey, whom he had seen that day in the store, and the two families became very good friends, though Mr. Whipple was so busy he did not have much time for calling.

One evening, however, Mr. Whipple came home from the store rather earlier than usual, and, finding Flossie and Freddie in his apartments playing with Laddie, the store-owner asked:

"How would you youngsters like to come and see a woodland camp—a camp with tents, a real fire, where a man is cooking his dinner and all that? How would you like it?"

"Oh, please take us!" begged Laddie.

"Where is it?" Freddie asked, ready to go at once.

"In my store," said Mr. Whipple.

"A store is a funny place for a camp in the woods," said Freddie. He and Flossie had often pretended to camp out in a tent made from a blanket or quilt, and they knew what it meant.

"Well, you just come and see it," laughed Mr. Whipple. "If your folks say it's all right, I'll take you all to-morrow."

"Oh, we'll come!" cried Freddie. "I love a camp!"

CHAPTER XV

SAD NEWS

Bert and Nan Bobbsey were so interested when they heard that Freddie and Flossie were going to see some sort of a camping scene at Mr. Whipple's store that they, too, begged to be allowed to join the party.

"Come right along!" exclaimed the merchant. "The more the merrier. I hope you'll like it."

"Is it a real camp, with trees and all?" asked Freddie.

"Well, there are some real bushes, and make-believe trees," said Mr. Whipple. "I couldn't grow real big woodland trees in my store, you know. But the tent is real, so is the fire, and the men who are camping out eat real food."

"I'd like that part," said Flossie.

"Well, come along, then," invited Mr. Whipple.

Mrs. Bobbsey, as well as Mrs. Whipple, were to go with the five children, and they made up a merry party as they set out for the uptown department store.

"Oh, we're going in an automobile!" cried Freddie, as they came out of the Parkview Hotel and saw a big car standing at the curb. The chauffeur got down off his seat and opened the door as he saw Mr. and Mrs. Whipple.

"Yes, this is our machine," said the merchant. "I don't care much for riding around New York, though in the Summer I take long trips in the car. But as we have so many children with us to-day," and he looked at Nan, Bert, Flossie, Freddie and Laddie, "it will be better to go in the machine."

On the way up, through the streets of the great city, the Bobbsey twins, as did Laddie, looked out of the windows at the many sights. Once Freddie saw a fire engine speeding on its way to some blaze.

"Oh, let's get out and watch!" he begged.

"Of course we can't do that!" said Mrs. Bobbsey.

"But maybe the fireman who rescued me

will be there," went on Freddie. "I'd like to see him again."

"I'll take you around to his fire house some time," promised Mr. Whipple. "Won't that do as well?"

Freddie thought it would, and then he noticed a street piano, on top of which perched a monkey.

"Maybe that's the one who tore your hat, Flossie," he said.

"No, this is a bigger one," returned the little girl. "Besides, if he is the same one I don't want to see him. I feel sorry about the nice cherries on my hat."

"Don't you like the one you and your brother bought in my store?" asked Mr. Whipple, with a laugh.

"Oh, yes, it's awful nice," said Flossie. "But it hasn't any *cherries* on it. But I like it just as well," she went on quickly, thinking, I suppose, that it might not be polite to say she did not.

"And now for the woodland camp!" cried Mr. Whipple, as they got out of his automobile in front of his store. "You see," he explained to Mrs. Bobbsey, "I sell a good many things that campers use—tents, pots, pans, fishing rods and lines, lanterns, axes, cook stoves, boats, canoes, guns and so on. Every year I set up, on the top floor of the store, a sort of woodland scene—a camp. I get real bushes from the woods and some logs. Then my men fix up a place to make it look as nearly like the real woods as we can. We have real moss and dirt on the ground, and a little spring of water. There is a real tent—two of them, in fact—and in one there are cots for sleeping, while in the other the meals are cooked.

"I hire some real campers to stay in my store camp, and they live almost as they would if they were actually camping out. This is to show the people how to use the camping things I sell. It is a new kind of advertisement, you see."

"And a very good one, I should think," said Mrs. Bobbsey.

"It sounds great!" cried Bert. "I wish we could go camping! Do you think we ever could, Mother?"

"Well, I don't know," answered Mrs. Bobbsey slowly. "I did hear your father say something about going to camp this Summer, but warm weather is a long way from us yet. We'll see."

"Oh, I believe we can go camping!" cried Nan to Bert in an excited whisper, as they entered the store elevator. "Won't it be wonderful?"

"Great!" said Bert. "I wouldn't want anything better than to camp on an island in some lake."

By this time they were up on the top floor of the big department store owned by Mr. Whipple, and at one end the twins and Laddie could see a number of persons.

"That's the camp," said Mr. Whipple. "I don't believe you've seen it this year, have you, Laddie?"

"No, Uncle Dan. Is it different from last year?" for the store-owner had the camp set up each Winter.

"Yes, it's a little different. There is a new kind of tent, and the men are different."

Mr. Whipple found a good place for the children to look in on the store camp. As he had said, there were the two tents, and, on some earth and moss between them, a real camp fire was burning, while a man, dressed just as you have seen campers in pictures, was cooking something in a pot over the blaze.

In one tent a table was set for a meal, and while the Bobbsey twins and the others looked on, the two men and a boy, who made up the store camping party, put their food on the table and began to eat.

They acted as though they were in a real camp, and as though they were not being watched by hundreds of eyes. They talked among themselves, washed their dishes after the dinner and then shot at a target with a small rifle, which sent out real bullets.

The boys—Bert, Freddie and Laddie—liked this part very much.

"It certainly looks like the real thing," was Bert's remark. "And the best part of it is, everything is so new and clean."

"It makes me feel hungry to look at 'em eat," was Laddie's comment.

"Oh, look at them shoot at that target!" cried Freddie excitedly. "I'd like to do that."

"You'd have to be careful, so that you didn't shoot yourself," replied his brother.

All about the tents in the store camp were things Mr. Whipple sold for those who wanted to take them to a real camp.

"There are some things here I'd like when I go camping," said Bert. "I'm going to ask my father to get them," he told Mr. Whipple.

"That will be nice. I asked your father to meet us here and have lunch," said the store owner, for there was a restaurant in his building. "I thought perhaps he'd like to see the camp himself."

"I'm sure he would," said Bert. "I hope he comes."

Then the Bobbseys and others looked at the camp some more, Bert being very much interested in a small canoe, which, he said, would be just right for him and Tommy Todd to paddle.

"Wouldn't you let me paddle with you?" asked Nan. "I know how—a little."

"Sure I'll let you," agreed her brother. "Oh, I do hope Dad will let us go camping!"

Mr. Bobbsey came in a little later, and he liked the store camp very much. He said he and his wife had talked of going to a camp in the Summer, and taking the children with them, but it was not all settled as yet.

"There's no better fun than camping out," said Mr. Whipple. "I used to do it when I was a boy, and I made up my mind that if ever I kept a store, which I always wanted to do, I'd sell camping things in it. And that's just what I'm doing," he added with a laugh.

"Doesn't this place make you think of our woods at home?" asked Nan of Bert.

"Yes, it does look like the woods around Lake Metoka," was his answer.

"And it's just like the place where Uncle Jack has his camp!" cried Freddie.

"Have the children an uncle who is a camper?" asked Mr. Whipple.

"No," answered Mr. Bobbsey, "but there is an old woodchopper, who lives in a log cabin near our town of Lakeport. He makes a living by chopping firewood. He lives all alone, and really sort of camps out. Every one calls him Uncle Jack. He was very good to Flossie and Freddie one day when they fell out of Bert's ice-boat.

"Poor Uncle Jack!" went on Mr. Bobbsey, with a sigh. "I am sorry to say I have bad news about him," he went on to his wife, but the children heard, though he spoke in a low voice.

"Uncle Jack!" cried Nan. "I hope he isn't dead!"

"No," answered her father, "but he is very ill, and he must go to a hospital, I am told. It's too bad about him."

CHAPTER XVI

THE BIG ELEPHANT

"What's the matter with Uncle Jack?" asked Mrs. Bobbsey, "and how did you hear about him, Richard?" she asked her husband.

"I had a letter from my bookkeeper," was the answer. "Before we came away I left word that the poor old man must be looked after, and I arranged to have news of him sent on to me. To-day I got a letter which says he is much worse than he has been, and really needs to go to a hospital. I think I shall have to raise the money to send him."

"Who is he?" asked Mr. Whipple. "I am interested. Who is this Uncle Jack?"

"He's just the nicest man!" cried Flossie. "He took us in when Freddie upset the ice-boat, and——"

"I didn't upset the ice-boat—it upset *itself!*" Freddie cried.

"Easy now, children! Don't dispute," said Mrs. Bobbsey gently.

"Uncle Jack is quite a character around Lakeport," went on Mr. Bobbsey. "I don't know all his story, but he has lived in the woods for a number of years. Where he was before that I don't know."

"He don't know hardly anything about his folks, Daddy!" piped up Freddie.

"How do you know?" asked Mr. Bobbsey.

"He told us so," put in Flossie. "It was that day he took us in his house, after we got spilled from the ice-boat."

"Well, perhaps that is right," said Mr. Bobbsey, when the two small twins had told what Uncle Jack had related to them. "They really know more about him than I do. All I know is that he is a good, faithful old man. He sells us wood and many of my friends buy of him. We help him all we can.

"I suppose he must have had *some* folks once upon a time, but, as he says, he has lost track of them. The bad news I have about him is that he needs to go to the hospital. I think he will not get well if he does not have a good doctor. He was so good to my children that I want to help him, and I am going to tell my bookkeeper to arrange for sending Uncle Jack where he can be taken care of. I'll pay the bill. He wouldn't take the money from me, but he won't know about this."

"Just a minute," said Mr. Whipple, as he led the way down to the restaurant in his store. "You say this old man lives in the woods?"

"Yes, he is a regular woodsman. He was a hunter and trapper once, I believe, though he has spent most of his life working for farmers. He loves now to live by himself in a sort of camp."

"I love camping myself," said Mr. Whipple, "and that is why I am so interested in selling things for campers. I love anybody who loves the woods, and, while I do not know this Uncle Jack, I'd like to help look after him."

"I shall be very glad to have you join me," said Mr. Bobbsey; and the twins, listening to this talk, though they did not understand all of it, knew that their old woodsman friend was going to be cured if it were found to be possible.

"We'll join each other in looking after him," went on Mr. Whipple. "You must let me pay half." And to this the children's father agreed. He said he would write back at once to his office, and tell some one there to look after the old woodchopper.

"Is there any other news from Lakeport?" Mrs. Bobbsey asked her husband at the restaurant dinner table, while the children were busy talking among themselves.

"No, not much. Everything is all right, I believe. I have some news for you, though, Bert," he went on, as his older son glanced across the table.

"What is it?" Bert questioned. "Did Tommy Todd go through the ice in the *Bird?*"

"No, but it has to do with the ice-boat. He went in a race in her on Lake Metoka, and, what is better, he won."

"Hurray for Tommy Todd!" cried Bert, so loudly that persons at other tables in the store dining room looked over and smiled, at which Bert's ears became very red.

"Did you hear anything of my friends?" asked Nan.

"No, my dear," answered her father. "And the reason I happened to have news for Bert was because Tommy's father wrote to me about some business matters, and Tommy slipped in a little note himself. Here it is, Bert."

It was just a little letter telling about the ice-boat, and Tommy expressed the wish that Bert would soon come home to help sail it in other races.

"I'd like to be back in Lakeport," said Bert, "but we're having such a good time here in New York I don't want to leave. Guess I'll write and tell Tommy so."

After dinner Mr. Whipple showed the Bobbseys and Laddie about the big store, and each of the children was allowed to pick out a simple gift to take away. Nan took a pretty ribbon; Bert a book he had long wanted; Flossie a piece of silk to make a dress for her doll, and Freddie saw in the toy department a little hose cart which, he said, was just what he wanted to go with his engine. Mr. Whipple gave it to Freddie, who was very much pleased. For his present from his uncle, Laddie picked out a little gun, which shot a cork.

"I can't break any of the hotel windows with this," he said to his aunt.

"Did you every break any windows?" asked Flossie, rather surprised.

"Once. I had a little wooden cannon that shot wooden balls. I shot one right through the window of our parlor, and the next ball hit George, the elevator boy, who was coming in with a telegram."

"And after that I had to take the cannon away from him," said Mrs. Whipple, with a smile. "But I think the cork pop-gun will be all right."

Never had the Bobbsey twins had as much fun as they did the day of their visit to Mr. Whipple's store. They were sorry when the late afternoon gave the signal for starting back home.

"But we'll have fun to-morrow," said Bert to Nan, as they reached their hotel.

"How do you know?" she asked.

"'Cause I heard Daddy tell Mother he was going to take us to Bronx Park to see the animals."

"Oh, will we see the monkeys?" cried Flossie, who heard what her older brother had said.

"Well, there are plenty of them there, so I've read," went on Bert. "Big ones, too."

"I like little monkeys best, even if one did pull my hat to pieces," went on Flossie. "Oh, I wish to-morrow would hurry up and come."

To-morrow finally did come, after the Bobbsey twins had gone to bed, though when it came it was to-day instead of to-morrow. But that's the way it always happens, doesn't it?

"All aboard for the Bronx!" cried Bert as, with his sisters and brother he followed Mr. Bobbsey into the subway train that would take them to the big animal park.

If ever you are in New York, I hope you will go to see this place. There are many strange animals in it, and it has beautiful birds and gardens also. Of course, when the Bobbsey twins went it was in Winter, and most of the animals had to be kept shut up in their cages in the warm houses. Some, however, like the deer, buffalo and other cattle, could stay out of doors even in cold weather.

There were so many things to see, even though it was Winter, when the park is not at its prettiest, that the Bobbsey twins hardly knew where to look first. Flossie and Freddie were anxious to get to the house where the monkeys were.

Some of the larger ones were uglier than they were funny, and in front of the cages were many persons who never seemed to tire of looking at the queer tricks the "four-handed" animals played on each other. You might say a monkey had five hands, for those that have tails certainly use them as much as they do their paws.

"Oh, look at that one big monkey, chewing a straw just like some of the men in front of the hotel at home chew toothpicks," said Nan, pointing to a chimpanzee crouched in a corner of his cage. He did, indeed, look like a little old man thoughtfully chewing on a toothpick. And he was so natural, and so much in earnest about it, that the Bobbsey twins, all four of them, burst out laughing.

This seemed to surprise the chimpanzee. He darted toward the front bars of his cage, shook them, as if in anger, and then ran into a corner, turning his back on the people.

"Just like a spoiled child," said Mrs. Bobbsey.

"Well, where shall we go next?" asked Mr. Bobbsey, for whenever he and his wife took the children on a little pleasure trip, the parents allowed the twins to choose their own places to go, and what to see, as long as it was all right.

"Let's go to see the elephants," cried Freddie. "I haven't seen any since we went to the circus."

"I want to see 'em too, and feed 'em peanuts!" added Flossie.

"No one is allowed to feed the animals in the park," said Mr. Bobbsey. "It isn't good for them to be eating all the while, and I suppose an elephant would keep on eating peanuts as long as you'd feed them to him. So we can't offer the big animals anything. They get all that is really good for them."

As it was cold, the elephants were all inside the big elephant house, with its several cages, in the front of which were heavy iron bars, set wide apart.

"They are close enough together to keep the elephants in," said Mr. Bobbsey, when his wife pointed out these bars, "though I suppose some animals might get out between them."

"Whew! they *are* big!" cried Freddie, when he stood close in front of one of the cages, or dens, and saw the elephant swaying to and fro back of the iron bars. "I wouldn't like one like him to step on me."

"I should say not!" laughed Bert. "Even a baby elephant would be too heavy. Look at this one stretch out his trunk to us. He wants something to eat, I guess!"

The big elephant, in front of whose barred cage the Bobbsey twins stood, did seem to be begging for something to eat.

Flossie had carried from the hotel a rosy-cheeked apple, which the waiter had given her at breakfast. Not wanting to eat it, she carried it with her to the park, and had it in her hand.

Now, for some reason or other, probably without thinking, she held it out to the elephant. The big animal saw what she was doing and turned toward Flossie.

"Oh, you mustn't feed the elephant!" cried Mrs. Bobbsey. "It's against the rules."

"I'm not feeding him, Mother," Flossie answered. "I'm just lettin' him *smell* it. It smells awful good!"

And just then the apple slipped from Flossie's hand and rolled or bounced straight into the elephant's cage, between the iron bars.

"Oh, my nice apple!" cried the little girl, and before any one could stop her she had crawled under the front rail, and had run in between the bars. Right into the cage of the big elephant ran Flossie after her apple.

CHAPTER XVII

CALLED HOME

FOR a moment Mr. Bobbsey, as well as his wife, was so surprised at what Flossie had done that neither could say or do anything. They just stood and looked at the little girl who was walking toward the apple, which lay in the straw just in front of the big elephant. Nan and Bert, however, together gave a cry of fear and Bert made a jump as though he intended to go into the elephant's cage, also.

His father, however, stepped in front of him, and said quietly:

"One child in there is enough at a time. I'll get Flossie!"

And Flossie, not at all thinking of danger, if danger there was, kept going on to get her apple.

The elephant, as it happened, was chained by one leg to a heavy iron ring in the side of his cage, and he could move only a short distance. But he was so anxious to get the apple that he stretched his legs as far as he could, pulling hard on the chain, and then he stretched out his trunk.

And truly it seemed made of rubber, that elephant's trunk did, from the way he stuck it out. But, stretch as he did, the elephant could not quite reach the apple, which he wanted very much.

"No, you mustn't take it!" Flossie was saying. "You can't have my apple! I was only going to let you smell it, Mr. Elephant. It isn't good for you to eat it, my mother says. I'll take it back and maybe some day I'll bring you another."

By this time Flossie was almost within reach of her red-cheeked apple, but, what was worse, she was also almost within reach of that trunk, which, however soft and gentle it might seem when picking up a peanut, was very strong, and could squeeze a big man or a little girl very hard indeed—that is, if the elephant was a bad one and wanted to do such a thing.

"Oh, Flossie! Come back! Come back!"

cried Mrs. Bobbsey, who had been so frightened at first that she could not say a word.

"I want to get my apple," answered the little girl. "The elephant can't have it! I only wanted to let him smell how good it would taste if he could eat it."

She was stooping over now, to pick up the fruit, and the tip of the long trunk was brushing the fluffy hair on Flossie's head. Nan covered her face with her hands, and Bert looked eagerly about, as though for something to throw at the big animal.

Mr. Bobbsey was climbing over the rail that was in front of the elephant's cage, and the people around were calling and shouting.

The elephant really did have the end of one of Flossie's curls on the tip of his trunk, when along came one of the keepers, or animal trainers. Somebody had sent him word that a little girl was in one of the animal cages. The keeper knew right away what to do.

"Back, Ganges!" he cried to the big elephant. "Get back there! Back! Back!"

The elephant raised his trunk high in the air, and made a funny trumpeting noise through it, as though half a dozen big men had all blown their noses at once. Then, as the keeper himself went in between the bars, the elephant slowly backed to the far end, his chain clanking as he did so.

"There! I got my apple!" cried Flossie, as she picked it up from where it had rolled in the straw. And then, before she knew what was happening, the keeper picked her up and carried her to the outside rail, where he placed her in Mr. Bobbsey's arms.

"Oh, Flossie! Flossie!" cried Mrs. Bobbsey, with tears in her eyes. "Why did you do it?"

"Why, I had to get my apple," answered the little girl. "Did you think the elephant would bite me?"

"He might," said Mr. Bobbsey, who was a little pale. "You must never do such a thing again, Flossie, no matter how many apples roll into elephants' cages."

"Oh, Ganges wouldn't have hurt her," said the keeper. "At least I don't believe he would, though he might have pinched her with his trunk if he had gotten the apple and she had tried to take it away from him. He's a very gentle elephant, and in the Summer many children ride on his back about the park."

"Oh, could I have a ride on his back?" asked Freddie, who had been anxiously watching to see what happened to Flossie.

"Not now, little man," answered the keeper. "It is too cold for the elephants to go out of doors now. If you're here in the Summer you and your sister may have lots of rides."

"Then I'm coming in the Summer!" cried Freddie.

"Oh, I don't believe I'd ever let you go near an elephant!" said Mrs. Bobbsey. "I was so frightened when I saw Flossie."

"There really wasn't any danger!" said the keeper again. "Here, I'll show you how gentle Ganges is."

The man went in the cage and the elephant, whose name was Ganges, seemed very glad to see his keeper. When the man called out an order the elephant lowered his trunk, made a sort of loop at one end, and when the keeper stepped in this the elephant raised him high in the air.

"I have taught him two or three tricks,"

said the man, coming back to the railing, outside of which stood the Bobbsey twins, their father and mother and a crowd of others who had heard what had happened. "He is a good elephant."

"Couldn't he have my apple?" asked Flossie. "I'm not so very hungry for it, and if I want one Daddy will get me another. Won't you, Daddy?" she asked, kissing her father, who was still holding her.

"I will if you promise never to go inside an elephant's cage again," he answered.

"Oh, I never will," said Flossie. "Here, you give him the apple," she said, holding it out to the keeper. "I guess he wants it."

"Oh, he *wants* it, all right!" laughed the man. "And, though it is not exactly according to the rules, I guess it will be all right this time. Here you are, Ganges!" he called. "Catch!"

The big elephant raised his trunk, making a sort of curling twist in it, and when the keeper threw the apple Ganges caught it as well as a baseball player could have done.

The next moment Flossie's apple was thrust into the elephant's mouth, and, as he chewed it, his little eyes seemed to twinkle in delight.

"He likes an apple just as much as I do," said Freddie. "Elephants is queer!"

"Don't try to go in there to feed this one peanuts!" said Bert, fearing that the little twin boy might try to do as his sister had done. Generally Flossie and Freddie wanted to do the same things.

"No, I won't go in," Freddie said.

Having swallowed the apple, the elephant held out his trunk toward the Bobbseys again. He was asking for "more," as plainly as though he had spoken.

"No more!" called the keeper, and this the elephant seemed to understand, for he lowered his trunk, and backed into his corner, throwing hay dust over his back as he did in the Summer to keep the flies from tickling him.

"Well, I guess we've seen enough of elephants for one day," said Mrs. Bobbsey. "I thought I should faint when I saw Flossie go into that cage. I wish I could get a cup of tea."

"We'll go and have lunch," said Mr. Bobbsey. "It's about noon, I think."

They went to a restaurant near a great round stone, which was perched on the top of a big ledge of rock, and when Freddie wanted to know what it was his father told him.

"That's a rocking stone," said Mr. Bobbsey. "It stands there on a sort of little knob, and it is so nicely balanced that a man, or two or three boys, can easily push it and rock it to and fro."

"Do you mean one man can move that big rock?" asked Bert.

"Yes, he can make it rock, but he can not make it move off the rock on which it rests. Come and try."

Bert and his father pushed their backs against the stone, and, surely enough, they could make it rock an inch or two back and forth. Freddie helped, or at least he thought he did, which is the same thing. But the stone really did rock, and the children thought it was quite a wonderful thing. Sometimes your heavy piano, if it stands on an uneven place in the floor, may be rocked back and forth a little. That's the way it was with the rocking stone. The restaurant where the Bobbseys ate was named "Rocking Stone," because it was within sight of the queer rock.

I have not time to tell you all that the Bobbsey twins saw and did in Bronx Park that day. But they had a fine time, and Flossie and Freddie, at least, wanted to come back the next day.

"There're lots of things that we didn't see," remarked Flossie.

"Yes. And I want to rock that big stone again," added Freddie. "Why, it rocked back and forth just as easy as a cradle!"

"Oh, Freddie Bobbsey! The idea! To make out that big rock was like a cradle!" cried Flossie.

"I didn't say *it* was like a cradle. I said it *wobbled* just like a cradle," replied Freddie. "Daddy, can we go back again to-morrow?"

"I planned to take you to the Natural History Museum to-morrow," said Mr. Bobbsey. "There you can see all sorts of stuffed animals —walruses almost as big as a small house, a model of a whale and many other queer things."

"Oh, do let's go!" begged Bert.

"We will," promised Mr. Bobbsey, but when the next day came the plan of the Bobbseys had to be changed.

In Mr. Bobbsey's mail that morning was a letter from his bookkeeper at the lumberyard, which, when Mr. Bobbsey had read it, made him thoughtful.

"I hope there isn't bad news," said Mrs. Bobbsey.

"No, not exactly *bad* news," was her husband's answer. "But I think I shall have to go back home."

CHAPTER XVIII

A QUEER RIDE

NAN and Bert, who were in the room with their mother and father when the letter was read, looked quickly at Mr. Bobbsey. Flossie and Freddie had gone to the next apartment to play with Laddie.

"Does that mean we've got to go back?" asked Bert.

"We haven't seen half enough of New York," added Nan.

"Oh, no, you won't have to come back with me," said Mr. Bobbsey. "You'll stay here at the hotel, and I'll return in a few days."

"What's it all about?" asked Mrs. Bobbsey.

"Uncle Jack," answered her husband.

"You mean the woodchopper who was so kind to Flossie and Freddie?"

"Yes, and because he was so kind I can't refuse to do what he wants me to."

"What is it he wants you to do?" asked Mrs. Bobbsey. "Did he write to you?"

"No, he got some one to do it for him, and my bookkeeper sent the letter on to me."

"But I thought Uncle Jack was going to the hospital," Bert said.

"So he is, Son. In fact, he is in the hospital now, but he is so ill that they fear he will not get better, even if the doctors do all they can for him. He is afraid he might die and he wants to see me before then. He says he has something he wants to tell me."

"What do you suppose it can be?" asked Mrs. Bobbsey.

"I haven't the least idea. Perhaps it's about his folks. He may have found some of them, or know where they are. If he has any relations they ought to know about him, and not leave him among strangers. Of course I'll do all I can for him. Mr. Whipple has given me some money to spend on Uncle Jack, so I think the poor old woodchopper will be all right, if he can only get well."

"Then you're going to see him?" asked Mrs. Bobbsey.

"Yes, I think I had better," answered Mr. Bobbsey. "He did me a great favor, caring for Flossie and Freddie, and I must do what I can for him. He says it will make his mind easier if he can talk to me before the doctors try to make him well in the hospital."

"Then we can't go to the Natural History Museum to-day!" exclaimed Nan.

"Oh, yes; your mother can take you."

"I fear I can't tell you, as well as Daddy can, about the different things," said Mrs. Bobbsey, smiling; "but I'll do the best I can."

"Oh, Momsey! Of course we love to have you!" cried Nan, kissing her mother.

"I know, but you want Daddy, too! I don't blame you. But we must give him up for a little while, if it is to help Uncle Jack."

"Oh, of course we will!" cried Nan, and Bert nodded his head to show that he agreed.

"I'll just about have time to catch a train for Lakeport," said Mr. Bobbsey, looking at his watch. "Where are Flossie and Freddie? I want to say good-bye to them."

"They are playing with Laddie," said Mrs. Bobbsey. "I'll get them."

The two younger Bobbsey twins felt sorry that their father had to go away, but they were told he would soon be back again. But as Flossie and Freddie were having such fun playing with Laddie, they did not really think much about Mr. Bobbsey going away, except for five minutes or so.

"Give our love to Uncle Jack," said Freddie, as he kissed his father, and started back for the Whipple rooms, where he and Laddie were building a bridge of books for the toy train of cars to cross a river, which was made of a piece of broken looking glass.

"And here's an extra kiss I'll give you for him," said Flossie, as she hugged her father in bidding him good-bye. "I love Uncle Jack."

So Mr. Bobbsey went back to Lakeport, and Mrs. Bobbsey got ready to take Nan and Bert to the Natural History Museum. At first it had been planned to take Flossie and Freddie, but, as they said they did not care much about stuffed animals, and as they were having such fun with Laddie, Mrs. Whipple told Mrs. Bobbsey she would look after the smaller twins and give them their lunch.

"Then I'll leave them with you," said the mother of Flossie and Freddie. "I hope they will be no trouble."

"I'm sure they'll be all right," said Laddie's aunt. "Don't worry about them."

So Flossie, Freddie and Laddie built the bridge of books, and on it safely ran the toy locomotive and cars over the river of shiny looking glass.

When they grew tired of this game they played automobile. To do that Laddie had to turn an old rocker upside down and stick on one leg a broken drum he had left from his Christmas toys. The drum was the steering wheel, and it made enough noise, when pounded on with a stick, to pretend it was an automobile horn.

Flossie and Freddie rode in the back part of the overturned chair, and Laddie sat in front of them and made believe he was a chauffeur of a taxicab, running about the streets of New York.

As Laddie knew the names of many places where the real taxicabs stop, he could call them out from time to time. So that Flossie and

Freddie went to the Grand Central Terminal, to Central Park, to the Public Library and many other places (make-believe, of course) in the queer pretend automobile.

"Oh, I'm going to stop off at the Public Liberry!" called out Flossie, while the play was going on.

"What you going to stop off at the Public Liberry for?" asked Freddie.

"I'm going to get a great big picture book," returned the little girl.

" 'Bout Cinderella?" questioned her brother.

"No. I'm going to get a picture book with all kinds of stories in it."

"We can't stop now!" yelled out Laddie. "We're three blocks past the liberry already."

"Well, then I won't bother," answered Flossie.

After that they played steamboat, a tin horn being the whistle, which was tooted every time the boat stopped or started. This game was great fun, and the children played it for some time until down in the street Laddie heard the tooting of fire engines and the clanging of bells.

"Oh, there's another fire!" he cried. "Let's go down to see it."

"No, indeed!" cried Mrs. Whipple, with a laugh, coming into the room just then. "No more fires for you boys. You can look out the window, but that's all."

And so they had to be content with that. The fire did not seem to be a large one, though it was somewhere near the hotel.

Down in the street were a number of engines and hose carts, and also two police automobile wagons, which had brought the officers who were to keep the crowd from coming so close as to get in the way of the fireman.

But there is not much amusement in looking out of a window at a fire which cannot be seen, and Flossie, Freddie and Laddie soon tired of this fun—if fun it was. Mrs. Whipple had left the room, to see a lady who called, when Freddie, taking a last look from the window to the street below, said:

"I know how we could have some fun!"

"How?" asked Laddie.

"Get in one of the police wagons and have a ride," went on the small Bobbsey boy.

"Oh, let's do it!" cried Flossie, always ready for anything that Freddie proposed. "How you going to do it?" she asked her brother.

"Why, we can go down in the elevator," Freddie said. "There's nobody in the police wagon now, for all the policemans are at the fire, but we can't see them or it. And the driver on the front seat of the wagon won't see us if we crawl in the back."

"Oh, so he won't!" cried Flossie. "'Member how we crawled in the empty ice-wagon once?" she asked Freddie.

"Yep. I tore my pants that day. But we had a nice ride. We'll have a nice ride now," he went on. "We can get in when they don't see us."

"But when the policemans comes back from the fire they'll see us and maybe arrest us," said Laddie in a whisper.

"They won't if we hide under the seats," returned Freddie. "See, there are long side seats in the police automobile wagon, and we can lie down under 'em and make believe we're in a boat."

"Oh, if it's a make-believe game, I'll do it," said Laddie. "I guess my aunt won't care, as long as it isn't goin' to a fire."

"Then come on," answered Freddie.

One of the police patrol wagons, or, to be more correct, automobiles, stood near the curb not far from the front entrance to the hotel. It had brought several policemen to the scene of the fire, and was waiting to take them back.

As Freddie had said, the chauffeur on the front seat could not see what went on in the back of the wagon, for there was a high board against which he leaned. And there were two long seats, one on each side of the auto patrol, under which three children could easily hide if the police were not too particular in looking inside their wagon as they rode back to the station house.

The three children hurried out into the hall and got in the elevator, which Laddie called to the floor by pressing the electric signal button.

"Am yo' all gwine far?" asked George, the colored elevator boy, as he shot up to the tenth floor and opened the door.

"I guess not very far," answered Freddie. None of them knew how long a ride they would get.

Out the front entrance of the hotel went the three tots. Because of the fire no one paid much attention to them, and the hotel help were used to seeing the children come and go, and perhaps thought Mr. and Mrs. Bobbsey, or Mrs. Whipple, were not far away.

So Flossie, Freddie and Laddie had no trouble in getting out, and then they walked quietly down to the automobile patrol. No one was near it, for automobiles—even police ones—are too common to look at in New York, especially when there is a fire around the corner, even if the blaze is a small one.

So, as it was, no one noticed the children climb into the patrol, and the driver, half dozing, did not hear them.

As Freddie had said, there was plenty of room for such small tots as these three to crawl under the long seats. And when they were stowing themselves away, Freddie found some blankets, which covered himself, his sister and Laddie.

"Now they can't see us!" said Freddie. "But we must keep still!"

"Hush!" cautioned Flossie. "Somebody's coming!"

And somebody was coming. It was the policemen coming back to take their places in the patrol, for the fire was out. Laughing and talking, they took their places on the long seat, never noticing the children hidden below.

And, a few seconds later, away started the automobile, taking the two Bobbsey twins and Laddie on a queer ride.

CHAPTER XIX

THE GOAT

EVERYTHING would have been all right if Flossie had not sneezed. At least that's what Freddie said afterward, and Freddie ought to have known, for he was right there. Laddie Dickerson did not say it was Flossie's fault, but then it is only brothers who say such things to their sisters. And Freddie did not really intend to make Flossie feel bad.

"But we might have had a bigger ride if you hadn't sneezed," said Freddie, after it was all over.

"Well, I couldn't help it," was what Flossie said. "And I guess you'd have sneezed, too, if that fuzzy blanket kept tickling your nose; so there!"

It was in the police patrol automobile that Flossie sneezed. With Freddie and Laddie, she was having a ride, you remember, the three children having hidden themselves under the seats, wrapped up in blankets, when the machine stood in front of the hotel while the policemen were at the fire.

For a time the two small Bobbsey twins and Laddie rode along in silence, the policemen not knowing the children were at their very feet. And after they had ridden about ten blocks, Flossie sneezed.

"A-ker-choo!" she cried, when a piece of the fuzzy blanket tickled her nose. "A-ker-choo!"

"Hello! What's that?" asked one of the policemen in the automobile.

"Sounded like a sneeze," said another.

"Sure it was a sneeze," came from a third.

"Maybe it was Mike, the chauffeur," suggested the first officer.

"It didn't sound like him," ventured a policeman, close to where the driver sat behind his wooden back-rest. "I say, Mike!" called the policeman, "did you sneeze?"

"Nope! Haven't time for sneezes now," answered the chauffeur.

"Then it was back here in this automobile," went on the first policeman, who was quite fat.

"Maybe it was a cat," suggested some one.

"Or a dog," added another.

Just then Freddie laughed—snickered would be more like what he did, I suppose—and once more Flossie sneezed. And Laddie snickered, too. They really could not help it any more than Flossie could help sneezing. For the two boys thought it very funny to listen to what the policemen were saying about Flossie's sneezes. And when the little girl's nose was tickled the second time by the fuzzy blanket, and she sneezed again, and the boys laughed—or snickered—the policemen knew where the noises came from.

"It's in here—right in our automobile!" said the fat policeman again.

"And it sounded right at my feet," added another.

Then all the policemen in the automobile leaned over and looked down. Even Flossie was laughing now, for it all seemed so funny, and she was wondering what her father and mother would say.

The laughter of the children made the blankets, under which they were hiding, shake as though the wind was blowing them, and seeing this one of the officers pulled loose one corner of the robe and there he saw Flossie, Freddie and Laddie.

"Well, I do declare!" cried a policeman with a red mustache. "It's children!"

"Three of 'em!" cried another.

The the two Bobbsey twins crawled from under the seat, and Laddie came with them, to stand up in the swaying automobile between the two rows of policemen.

"Where in the world did you come from?" asked one officer.

"Under there," answered Freddie, and he pointed to the place where the blankets were still rolled up.

"And how did you get there?"

"We crawled in to get a ride," said Flossie, "and I couldn't help sneezing. That fuzzy blanket tickled my nose so!"

The policemen laughed at this.

"But who are you and where do you belong?" asked one of the officers who, having some stripes on his sleeve and some gold lace on his cap, seemed to be the leader.

"We're part of the Bobbsey twins," said Freddie. "The other half of us—that's Nan and Bert—have gone to see a stuffed whale."

"No, the whale isn't stuffed—it's the sea lion, or wallyrus—I forget which," put in Flossie. "The whale's only made out of plaster and wood."

"Well, anyhow, Nan and Bert are there," said Freddie.

"And you're here," said the red-mustached policeman. "That's easy to see, though what he means about being half of the Bobbsey twins is more than I can guess. How many is twins, anyhow?"

"Two," some one said.

"We're four—that is, two sets," explained Flossie painstakingly. "Bert and Nan are older than us."

"Oh, I see," said the policeman whom the other officers called Captain, or "Cap." for short. "Well, where did you come from and where are you going?"

"We live at the Parkview Hotel," said Freddie, "and we got in here to have a ride. We didn't think you'd find us so soon."

"It *is* too bad," said the captain, with a laugh. "And I'm afraid I can't give you a ride any farther than to the station house. I suppose you know who you are and where you live," he went on, with a smile; "but, as we have to do things by rule in the police department, I'll have to make sure. So I'll take you to my office and telephone to the hotel. If I find you belong there I'll take you back."

"Then we'll have another ride!" said Flossie. "That will be nice, won't it, Freddie?"

"Um, I guess so. Only I'd like to sit out in front with the driver as long as you sneezed and told 'em we were here."

"I didn't sneeze any more than you giggled!" cried Flossie. "And, anyhow, I couldn't help it. That fuzzy blanket——"

"Of course, that was it!" laughed the captain. "Never mind. No harm has been done, and you shall have a ride back home. Though I think, for the sake of your folks, I'll send you back in a taxicab, instead of in this patrol auto, and with an officer in plain clothes, instead of one wearing a uniform. It will look better at the hotel," he explained to his men.

"Sure," was their answer.

And so the two little Bobbsey twins and Laddie were given a ride to the precinct station house in the big automobile patrol, and they sat on the laps of the kindly policemen.

Quite a crowd of children gathered around the doors of the police station as Flossie, Freddie and Laddie were lifted out of the automobile, and there were all sorts of stories told about them. Some believed the children had been rescued from the fire; others that they had been taken from a robbers' cave, and still others that these were the children, who, playing with matches, had caused the fire.

But all these guesses were wrong, as we know. Flossie, Freddie and Laddie had just gone for a ride, and they had one, though it did not turn out exactly as they expected. However, they had a good time.

It did not take the police captain long to find out that what Freddie had said was true—that the three youngsters lived at the Parkview Hotel.

"Your aunt has been looking all over for you," said the captain to Laddie, after telephoning. "I sent word that I'd soon have you safely back, and you mustn't run away again."

"I asked him to," said Freddie, telling the truth like a little man. "I asked him and Flossie to come."

"Well, next time you'd better ask before you crawl into a police automobile," said the captain, with a laugh. "You can't always tell where it is going. However, no harm is done this time. Come and see me again," he added.

Then the captain called a taxicab and sent the children to the hotel in charge of one of his policemen, who did not wear a uniform. This was done so no crowd would gather in front of the hotel to stare at Freddie, Flossie and Laddie, as would have happened if a policeman in uniform, with his bright brass buttons, had gone with them.

"Oh, Laddie! how could you do it and worry me so?" cried Mrs. Whipple, when her little nephew had come back to the hotel with the Bobbsey twins.

"I asked him," said Freddie, willing to take all the blame. "We wanted a ride and we just crawled in and hid. I'm awful sorry."

"And I'm sorry I sneezed," said Flossie. "If I hadn't maybe we'd have had a longer ride."

"No, we wouldn't," declared Freddie, shaking his head. "We got to the station house, anyhow, and that's where the automobile lives when it isn't workin'. Anyhow, we had fun!"

"Yes, we did," said Laddie; "and I liked it."

"But you mustn't go away again without telling me," said his aunt.

"I won't," he promised.

"Next time we'll take you with us," said Flossie. "You'll like it, only I hope a fuzzy blanket doesn't make you sneeze."

So the Bobbsey twins, with their little friend, had a ride away and a ride back again, and when Mrs. Bobbsey came home that afternoon from the Natural History Museum with Bert and Nan, and heard what had happened, she was so surprised she did not know what to say.

Of course she made Flossie and Freddie promise never to do it again, and of course they said they never would.

"I never saw such little tykes as Flossie

and Freddie have gotten to be lately," said Mrs. Bobbsey to Nan that night.

"This being in a big city seems just to suit them, though," returned Nan.

"Yes. But I wish your father would come back. I feel rather lost without him in this big hotel."

"I'm here," said Bert, with a smile.

"Yes, you'll have to be my little man, now. And do, please, keep watch of Flossie and Freddie while your father is away. There's no telling what they'll do next."

And really there was not. For instance, who would have supposed that a goat——

But there, I'd better start at the beginning of this part of my story.

It was a few days after the ride in the automobile patrol that Mrs. Bobbsey received word that a friend whom she had known when they were both small children was living in New York. This lady asked Mrs. Bobbsey to call and see her.

"We do not live in a nice part of New York," wrote the lady—who was a Mrs. Robinson—in her letter, "for we can't pay much rent. But our apartment house is not hard to reach from your hotel, and I would very much like to see you. Come and bring the children. They can watch the other children playing in the streets. I know the streets are not a very nice place to play in, but that's all we have in New York."

So Mrs. Bobbsey decided to call on her old friend, whom she had not seen for many years. She said she would take Flossie and Freddie with her. Nan and Bert were going to a moving picture show with another boy and girl and the latter's mother.

Mrs. Robinson lived on the east side of New York, in what is called an apartment house. Some called them tenements, and in them many families are crowded together, for room is very valuable in the big city of New York.

After Mrs. Bobbsey had talked for a while with her former girlhood friend, Flossie and Freddie, who had been sitting still in the parlor, asked if they could not go out in the street and watch the other children at play.

"I WISH WE HAD A GOAT," SAID FREDDY.

The Bobbsey Twins in a Great City. *Page* 216

"Yes, but don't go off the steps," said their mother.

The two Bobbsey twins promised, but something happened that made them forget. This was the sight of a red-haired, snub-nosed boy, driving a goat, hitched to a small wagon, up and down the street.

"Oh, look at that!" cried the excited Freddie. "Isn't that great!"

"It's cute," said Flossie. "I wonder if he'd give us a ride?"

"Let's ask him," said Freddie. "I've got ten cents. Maybe he'd ride us for that. Come on!"

And so, forgetting all about their promise not to go off the steps of the apartment house where their mother's friend lived, the two small Bobbsey twins hurried down to look at the goat.

CHAPTER XX

MR. BOBBSEY COMES BACK

"HEY, Jimmie! Give us a goat ride, will you?" called a boy in the street.

"I will for two cents," answered the red-haired lad driving the goat and wagon.

"Aw, go on. Give us a ride for a cent!"

"Nope. Two cents!"

"Oh, did you hear that?" asked Flossie of Freddie. "He gives rides for two cents."

"Then we'll have some," said Freddie. "How many rides can you get for ten cents?"

"A lot, I guess," said Flossie, who forgot all about the number-work she had studied for a little while in school.

"Hey!" called Freddie to the boy with the goat. "We've got two cents—we want a ride."

The boy, who was sitting in an old goat wagon, pulled on the reins and guided his animal over toward the curb.

"Does you really want a ride?" he asked. "No foolin'?"

"No foolin'," answered Freddie. "Sure we want a ride. I've got five cents." He showed only half of the money he had in his pocket, keeping the other nickel back.

"I'll give you an' your sister a ride for dat!" cried the goat boy, not speaking the way Freddie and Flossie had been taught to do. "Hop in!"

"Can I drive?" asked Freddie.

"Nope. I'm afraid to let youse," was the answer. "Billy's a good goat, but you see he don't just know you. Course I could introduce youse to him, an' then he'd know you. But first along you'd better not drive him. I'll steer him were you want to go. I gives a ride up an' down de block fer two cents," he went on. "Course two of you is four cents."

"I've got a nickel," said Freddie quickly.

"Sure, dat's right. I forgot. Well, I'll give you both a ride up and down de block and half way back again for de nickel."

"Here it is," said Freddie, handing it over, as he and Flossie took their seats in the goat wagon. There was plenty of room for them and the red-haired driver. Other children on the block crowded to the curbstone and looked on with eager eyes as the Bobbsey twins started on their ride. Mrs. Bobbsey, talking with her friend in the darkened parlor, knew nothing of what was going on.

"Say, he is a good goat," said Freddie, when they were half-way down the block.

"Sure he's a good goat!" agreed the boy, whose name was Mike. "There ain't none better."

"It's lots of fun," said Flossie.

It was a fine day, even if it was Winter. The sun was shining brightly, so it was not cold. What snow there was in New York, before the Bobbseys came on their visit, had either melted or been cleaned off the streets so one would hardly know there had been a storm.

"I wish we had a goat," said Freddie, when the ride was almost over.

"So do I," agreed Flossie. "Let's ask Daddy to buy one," she suggested.

"We will," said Freddie.

"I'm goin' to sell dis goat," put in Mike.

"You are? Why?" cried the Bobbsey twins.

"'Cause I'm going to work. You see I won't have time to look after him. I bought him off a feller what moved away, an' I keeps de goat in Sullivan's livery stable. But I have to pay a dollar a month, an' so I began givin' de boys an' girls around here rides for two cents to pay for Billy's keep. But I can't do dat when I goes to work, so me mudder says I must sell 'im. I don't want to, but I has to."

Flossie looked at Freddie and Freddie looked at Flossie on hearing this. Neither of them said a word, but any one who knew them could easily have told that they were thinking of the same thing—the goat.

"Well, I'll ride you back to where youse got in me wagon," said Mike, "and then your nickel's about used up."

"Oh, I've got another!" cried Freddie eagerly. "We want more ride. Don't we, Flossie?"

"Sure we do! Oh, it's such fun!"

So they rode up and down the block again, and when that was over Flossie and Freddie spent some time talking to Mike.

By this time Mrs. Bobbsey had ended her visit and had come out to look for her children.

"I thought I told you not to go off the steps," she said. They were down the street looking at the goat.

"Well, we didn't mean to," admitted Freddie. "But we did so much want a goat ride."

"And we had ten cents' worth!" laughed Flossie.

Mrs. Bobbsey smiled. It was very hard to be cross with these small twins. They never meant to do wrong, and, I suppose, taking a ride up and down the block was not so very bad.

"Good-bye!" called Freddie to Mike, the goat boy, as Mrs. Bobbsey led her children away.

"Good-bye!" added Flossie, waving her hand.

"Good-bye," echoed Mike.

"And don't forget!" said Freddie.

"No, I won't."

Mrs. Bobbsey might have asked what it was Mike was not to forget, only she was in a hurry to get back to the hotel, and so did not question Freddie.

When they reached their rooms they found a letter from Mr. Bobbsey, saying he would have to stay in Lakeport a day longer than he expected. But he would soon be in New York again, he wrote.

Bert and Nan came home from the moving pictures, saying they had had a delightful time.

"So did we—in a goat wagon," cried Freddie.

"And Freddie and me are goin' to——" began Flossie, but Freddie quickly cried:

"Come on and play fire engine, Flossie!" so his little sister did not finish what she had started to say.

It was the next day, soon after breakfast, that one of the hotel messengers—a small colored boy—knocked on the door of the suite of apartments occupied by the Bobbsey family, and when Mrs. Bobbsey answered, the colored boy said:

"He am downstairs, Ma'am. He am in de lobby."

"Who is?" asked Mrs. Bobbsey.

"De boy what wants to see yo' little boy, Ma'am."

"Some one to see Freddie? Who is it?"

"I don't know, Ma'am. He didn't gib no name."

"Oh, perhaps it is Laddie," said Mrs. Bobbsey. "Bert, please go down and see, will you? If it's Laddie, who wants Freddie to play with him, I don't see why he didn't come here. But go and see."

"Oh, I know who it is," said Freddie. "You don't need to go, Bert. Just give me five dollars, Mother, and I'll buy him."

"Buy him? Buy what?" asked the surprised Mrs. Bobbsey. "What in the world are you talking about, Freddie?"

"Mike, the goat boy. He's brought Billy here, I guess, and Flossie and I are going to buy him. Can't we, please?"

"What? Buy a goat when we're stopping at this hotel?" cried his mother. "Bert, do go and see what mischief those children have gotten into now. A goat! Oh, dear!"

"I'll go with him, 'cause Mike don't know Bert," offered Freddie.

"And I want to come!" said Flossie. "I want to see our goat."

"Your goat!" cried Nan.

"Yes, we're going to buy him. Mike brought him to sell to us."

And that is what had happened. When Mrs. Bobbsey followed Bert and Freddie down to the hotel lobby, leaving Nan to look after Flossie in the rooms, this is what she saw:

Out at the side entrance to the hotel was the goat and the rickety express wagon, in charge of a red-haired, snub-nosed boy, Mike's small brother. Mike himself, rather ragged, but clean and neat enough, was in the lobby, sitting at his ease on one of the big leather chairs, waiting.

"I've brought de goat," he said to Freddie, as soon as he saw that small Bobbsey with Bert.

"What does it all mean?" asked Mrs. Bobbsey, while a crowd of the hotel guests and help gathered about.

"Why, your little boy, Ma'am, what I rode in me goat wagon up and down our block, said you'd buy Billy when I was ready to sell him.

I'm ready now, 'cause I'm goin' to work. So I brought de goat an' wagon here to de hotel, just as your little boy made me promise to do. It'll be five dollars for de goat."

For a moment Mrs. Bobbsey did not know what to say. Then she turned to Freddie and asked:

"Did you really tell him you'd buy his goat, Freddie?"

"I said you'd buy it for Flossie and me. Won't you? We can have such fun with it!"

"A goat in a New York hotel!" cried Bert, laughing. "Oh, dear!"

"Hush, Bert," said his mother. "Freddie did not know any better. Of course we can't keep it," she said to Mike, "and I'm sorry you had the trouble of bringing him here. My little boy didn't stop to think, I'm afraid. He should have told me. But here is a dollar for your trouble, and I think you can easily sell your goat somewhere else."

"Oh, yes, I can easy sell him," said Mike. "But your little boy made me promise to bring Billy to dis hotel to-day and here I am, 'cordin' to promise."

"Yes, I see you kept your word," and Mrs. Bobbsey could not help smiling. "But really we have no place to keep a goat here, and we could hardly take it to Lakeport with us. So I'm afraid Freddie will have to do without it."

"All right," said Mike good-naturedly, as he took the dollar.

Of course Freddie and Flossie were disappointed at not having the goat and wagon, but they soon forgot that when their mother promised to take them to see another play that afternoon.

"It's a wonder Flossie or Freddie didn't try to bring the goat up to our rooms in the elevator," said Bert, when they were in their apartment again.

"Well, he was a good goat!" declared Freddie.

"And he could go fast," added Flossie.

"I was going to play fireman with him when we got back to Lakeport," went on Freddie. "Now I can't."

"I think you'll have just as much fun some other way," said his mother, laughing.

Three days after that, when Mrs. Bobbsey

came in from shopping with the two sets of twins, she heard some one moving about in their apartment as she entered.

"Oh, it's Daddy!" cried Flossie, as some one caught her up in his arms. "Daddy's come back!"

"I'm so glad!" called Freddie, running to get a hug and kiss from his father. "And we almost had a goat!" he added.

CHAPTER XXI

UNCLE JACK'S REAL NAME

"WELL! Well!" laughed Mr. Bobbsey, when he heard what Freddie said. "That's great! Almost had a goat, did you? I must hear about that!"

"But first tell us about Uncle Jack," begged Nan. "Is he going to get better?"

"Oh, I hope he is going to get better!" broke in Freddie. "It isn't a bit nice to be sick. You have to stay in bed, and sometimes you have to have your head all bound up, and sometimes you have to take the awfullest kind of medicine ever was."

"You don't always have to stay in bed when you're sick," put in Flossie. "And sometimes the medicine isn't bad a bit. It's sweet and nice."

"But tell us about Uncle Jack," begged Nan again. "He'll get better, won't he?"

"That is something the doctors can't tell," answered her father. "I saw him in the hospital."

"Was he glad to see you?" asked Mrs. Bobbsey.

"Well, to tell you the truth he didn't know me. He was very ill and was out of his head with fever. I did what I could for him, and saw that he would be well taken care of, and then went to Mr. Todd's house to stay all night. I said I'd go back to the hospital in the morning, but Uncle Jack was no better, and after waiting two or three days, I decided to come back here."

"Didn't he know you at all?" asked Nan.

"No, he was out of his head with fever all the while. Before I came, he had told some of the doctors that he had something very important to tell me—something that had to do with his friends or relations, they said. He would tell no one else but me, but when I got to his bedside he could not talk so that I could understand him. So really I don't know any more about him than before. I don't even know what his real name is.

"Sometimes he used to call himself Jackson, and again it would be some other name. I think he may not have known who he really was. But if he does, it will be some time before he can tell me, or any one else. He was still out of his head when I came away."

"Are you going back?" asked Mrs. Bobbsey.

"Not until they send for me, which will be when he takes a turn for the better or worse. I want to do all I can for the poor old man, for he was so good to Flossie and Freddie. But now tell me about the goat."

Freddie and Flossie took turns doing that, and a very funny story they made of it, too. Mr. Bobbsey laughed, and laughed again. Then he had to hear about everything else that had happened while he was in Lakeport.

"And now tell us what happened there—I mean besides about Uncle Jack," said Nan. "Did you see any of my friends?"

"And did you see Bessie Benton?" Flossie asked, naming a little girl with whom she often played.

"Yes, I saw Bessie," said Mr. Bobbsey, "and she sent you her love."

"Did you see Tommy Todd?" Freddie queried.

"Yes; I stayed at his house."

"How is the ice-boat?" asked Bert.

"Well, there has been a thaw, as you know, and there isn't enough ice in Lake Metoka on which to sail the *Bird*. I guess Tommy'll have to wait until you get back there, Bert. We'll have more cold weather yet."

"Oh, are we going to leave New York?" asked Nan sorrowfully.

"We can't *live* here," said her mother. "We've stayed longer now than I thought we would. Have you much more business to look after?" she asked her husband.

"It will take about two weeks more, and then I think we'll go back to Lakeport. But you children can have plenty of good times in two weeks, I should think."

"Of course we can!" cried Bert. "And when we get back home——"

"Are we going camping?" interrupted Freddie. "Flossie and I want to go camping in the woods."

"On an island in a lake," added the little

girl. "And we can take the bugs that go around and around and around and—and——"

"And the bugs that go around and around will catch all the mosquitoes that fly up and down, up and down, and bite us!" laughed Mrs. Bobbsey. "Yes, we certainly shall have to take the 'go around' bugs to camp with us, children."

"Do you really think we can go camping?" asked Bert of his father.

"Well, I don't know. We'll see."

The Bobbsey twins, both sets of them, did indeed have many more good times in New York. I wish I had room to tell you about them, but I have not space. They went to see many sights, paid another visit to Central Park and Bronx Park and saw many nice plays and moving picture shows.

Mr. and Mrs. Whipple and Laddie often went with the Bobbseys on little excursions about the great city. Laddie and the children became better friends than before, and Mrs. Whipple said her little nephew had never had such good times in all his life.

"He missed his mother greatly before your

children came to this hotel," said Mrs. Whipple to Mrs. Bobbsey.

"When is Mrs. Dickerson coming back from California?" asked Mrs. Bobbsey.

"When it is warm here. She can not stand cold weather. But she did not go out to California altogether on account of the climate."

"Didn't she?"

"No. You have heard my husband speak of a long-lost brother—also a brother of Mrs. Dickerson's, who was a Whipple before her marriage."

"Yes, I heard something about that."

"Well, for a number of years my husband and Mrs. Dickerson have been trying to find this lost brother. And there was a rumor that he had gone to California when a boy and had grown up among the miners near San Francisco. It was to find out, if possible, whether or not this was so, that Mrs. Dickerson went out West. Though, to be sure, the Winters here are hard for her to endure."

"Did she have any success in finding her brother?" asked Mr. Bobbsey.

"No," answered Mrs. Whipple, "she did not,

I'm sorry to say. She and my husband feel bad about it. But he may be found some day. He has been missing many years."

It was two or three days after this talk that, one evening, Mr. and Mrs. Whipple and Laddie were in the hotel rooms of the Bobbseys, paying a visit, when a telegram was brought up for Mr. Bobbsey.

"It's from Lakeport," he said, as he opened it and saw the date and the name of the place from which it had come.

"From Lakeport?" asked Mr. Whipple, as Mr. Bobbsey was reading the message. "That's where the old woodsman lives, isn't it?"

"Yes," answered Mrs. Bobbsey. "And, though he is very ill, he is being well looked after, thanks to the money you gave for him."

"Oh, I didn't give much. It was your husband who did the most. I was glad to help, for I always have a soft spot in my heart for those who camp in the woods. How is Uncle Jack, by the way? I believe that's his name?"

"Yes, that *was* his name," said Mr. Bobbsey in a queer voice, as he held the telegram out to Mr. Whipple.

"It was his name—what do you mean?"

"I mean that he has come to his senses now. The doctors have operated on him and he will get better. There was an injury to his head that made him forget much of his early life. But now he is all right and he remembers his real name."

"What is it?" asked Mrs. Bobbsey, while the others breathlessly waited for an answer. "What is his real name?"

"John Whipple," was the answer. "That's what this telegram is about. Though everybody called the woodchopper Uncle Jack, his real name is John Whipple!"

CHAPTER XXII

REUNITED

THE Bobbsey twins were not as much surprised at what their father said, after reading the telegram, as was Mr. Whipple. He fairly jumped up from his chair, on hearing what Mr. Bobbsey answered, and reached out his hand for the message.

"His name is Whipple!" cried the department store owner. "Are you sure his name is John Whipple?"

"That's what the telegram says," went on Mr. Bobbsey. "You may read it. It seems he asked to have it sent to me as soon as he knew he was getting better, and when he remembered who he was. He says he remembers he had a brother and a sister."

Mr. Whipple seemed very much excited. Even Flossie and Freddie, young as they were, could tell that. He took the telegram from Mr. Bobbsey, but he did not read it. Instead he looked at the children's father and asked:

"Do you know this old woodchopper very well?"

"I have seen him a number of times," said Mr. Bobbsey, "and he often comes to my house with loads of wood. The children know him, too. I have told you how he helped Freddie and Flossie out of the snow bank and took them to his cabin."

"What sort of looking man is he?" the store owner questioned eagerly.

Mr. Bobbsey described Uncle Jack's looks, and also told of his having come to Lakeport a number of years before, from where, no one knew. He made friends and lived in the woods. That was all that was known about him. Few, if any, had known his name until now.

"And so he is John Whipple," said Mr. Bobbsey, rather talking to himself than to any one else. "Strange that he should have forgotten it all these years. I wonder if I can find his folks. Why, your name is Whipple!" he said to Laddie's uncle. "Do you know who Uncle Jack might be?"

"I think I do," said Mr. Whipple slowly, and his voice trembled. "I think he is my long-lost brother, and the brother of my sister—he is Laddie's other uncle! Oh, if it only turns out that way!"

"Is Uncle John found?" asked Laddie, who, with his playmates, Flossie and Freddie, began to understand a little of what was going on. "Is Uncle John found?"

"We hope so, my dear," said his aunt gently. "How can we make sure?" she asked her husband.

"There is only one way," he said.

"You mean to go to Lakeport?"

"That's it. Where can I find him?" asked Mr. Whipple of Mr. Bobbsey. "Uncle Jack, I will call him, until I make sure he is my long-lost brother," he added.

"He was taken to a private hospital, not far out of town. I'll be very glad if you and your wife, and Laddie, as well, will come back to Lakeport with us. Then you can see Uncle Jack and make sure whether or not he is your brother."

"I'll be glad to do that. But I thought you

were going to stay in New York for some time yet."

"We can go back to-morrow if need be," said Mr. Bobbsey. "My business is now in good shape, and I can come back here if there is any call for me."

"Oh, let's all go back to Lakeport!" cried Freddie. "Maybe then we can have a goat, Flossie."

"Oh, may we, Mother?" the little girl demanded.

"I'll buy 'em a goat—two goats—if this news proves true," said Mr. Whipple. "Oh, I do hope I have found my brother!"

"How did he get lost?" asked Mrs. Bobbsey.

"It happened when my sister and I were very little children. John was somewhat older. Our parents died, and distant relatives, living far away from our home, took charge of my sister and me. John, who was a half-grown boy, stayed with the family of a neighboring farmer, who had been friends of our parents, and the relatives took my sister and me away with them.

"Shortly after this the farmer lost his money, his farm, everything, and soon after moved away, taking John with them. News of this did not come for some time to our relatives, and when it did and they began a search for John, all trace of him was lost. They learned that the farmer had died in a public hospital in a strange city, and all trace of his widow and John was lost right there.

"When I became old enough, I started to look for John, but could not find him. My sister could not, either, though lately she heard he was in California, but it was not true. And so, for many years, we have been trying to find John Whipple. And at last I know where he is!"

"Let us hope Uncle Jack is your brother," said Mr. Bobbsey gently.

"We will soon know," said Mrs. Whipple.

The stay of the Bobbseys in the great city of New York came to a sudden end, but they had had a good time, and might come again some time. Besides, Mr. and Mrs. Whipple were going back with them, to see if the old woodchopper were really the long-lost man, and

Flossie and Freddie thought that almost as good as if they had stayed in the city.

"And Laddie is coming, too!" cried Freddie. "We'll have heaps of good times."

"And maybe we'll get a goat," said Flossie. "If we do, I'm going to drive him sometimes."

"Yes, you can," agreed Freddie.

Mr. Bobbsey closed up most of his New York business matters, and Mr. Whipple, with his wife and Laddie, got ready to go to Lakeport with the Bobbseys. Word was sent to Dinah, the fat cook, and her husband, Sam, to get the Lakeport house ready for the family and for the Whipples, who would stay with them for a short time.

Another telegram came from the hospital about Uncle Jack. It said he was doing well, and that his mind was clear. He was certain he was John Whipple, and that he had relations somewhere. But, for fear there might be a disappointment, after all, no word was sent him about Mr. Daniel Whipple's coming on. Nor was Laddie's mother, in California, told. They wanted to make sure there would be no mistake.

Once more the Bobbsey twins were in the big Pennsylvania station, and Freddie almost made the whole party miss the train by stopping in the arcade to show Laddie where the bugs, that went "around and around and around," had been bought.

"See what beautiful colors they are!" exclaimed Freddie. "Green and blue and red and brown and pink and yellow and—and—oh, every kind!"

"And you ought to see how fast some of 'em go around!" exclaimed Flossie. "They just keep on going around and around and around till sometimes you can't most see 'em go!"

"And you wind 'em just like this——" explained Freddie, making a queer little movement wih his chubby hand.

"Oh, I know just how they go," said Laddie. "Didn't I see yours run?"

"Come, children, we'll have to hurry," said Mr. Bobbsey. "We don't want to miss the train."

"I want some of those bugs," said Laddie wistfully.

"We can get some later," replied his aunt.

"But they may be all gone when we come back!"

"I don't think so," his aunt replied. "See! They have a whole store full of them." And then the crowd hurried off to catch the train.

In due time they arrived in Lakeport, and when Flossie and Freddie rushed into the house, almost knocking down dear old fat Dinah, they found Splash, the big dog, waiting for them. And Splash did really knock Flossie down, he was so glad to see her. But she was so fat that, really, falling just to the floor did not hurt her at all. And, anyhow, she sat down on the tail of Splash, so it was like a cushion, only, of course, he could not wag it until Flossie got up.

"Oh, chilluns! how glad I is t' see yo' all!" cried Dinah, trying to hug all four of them at once.

"And here's Laddie," said Flossie. "Aren't you glad to see him?"

"Co'se I is, chile! I lubs yo' all!" and she hugged Laddie, too.

Leaving his wife at the Bobbsey home, Mr.

Whipple went with Mr. Bobbsey to the hospital where Uncle Jack (as they still called him) had been taken.

The old woodchopper was much better, though still weak and ill. One of the doctors had told him some one was coming to see him, and had said it might prove to be some one who knew about his brother and sister. Poor Uncle Jack's eyes filled with tears.

"Oh, I only hope it is true," he said.

Mr. Whipple walked softly into the hospital room. After a short talk with the old woodchopper, Mr. Daniel Whipple cried:

"It is true! I am your brother! Oh, John, I have found you at last!"

There was no doubt of it. After further talking it over between them, Mr. Daniel Whipple and Mr. John Whipple made sure they were brothers. And when Uncle Jack (as many still kept on calling him) got better, every one could see that he and Mr. Whipple, the department store owner, looked very much alike, except that the woodchopper was older.

But I must not call him a woodchopper, for he was that no longer.

"You are coming to live with me," said his brother Dan. "I have enough to look after you. No more hard work for you!"

"I am very happy," said Uncle Jack. "Bless the dear children; they helped you to find me as much as any one did."

"Yes," said Uncle Dan, as the Bobbsey twins called Laddie's uncle, "if Flossie and Freddie hadn't fallen off the ice-boat I might still be looking for you, John."

And so, as you have read, everything came out all right. Uncle Jack, in a few weeks, was able to leave the hospital, quite well again, though he was very weak, and he was old. He grew stronger in time, but of course no younger, though he lived for a number of happy years with his brother.

Laddie stayed in Lakeport over two weeks, and he had many good times with the Bobbsey twins. His mother, as soon as the weather became warm, came on from California and said she had never seen Laddie play with two children he liked more than he did Flossie and Freddie. Bert and Tommy Todd sailed the ice-boat, and it did not upset again, though once it came very near it. Flossie and Freddie were given the cart and goat they so much wanted, but I shall have no room here to tell about the fun they had with them.

"Well, it certainly was a dandy Winter," remarked Bert one day, when the air felt like Spring.

The Whipples, taking Uncle Jack with them, had gone back to New York, and the Bobbseys were alone.

"It will soon be Summer," said Nan. "I wonder what we shall do then. Where are we going to spend our vacation, Mother?"

"Oh, I think Daddy has some nice place picked out."

"Let's try to guess!" said Nan to Bert.

But they did not easily do that, and as I do not want to keep you guessing, I will say that the children did have a fine time that Summer.

Where they went, and what they did while there, you may find out by reading the next book of this series, to be called, "The Bobbsey Twins on Blueberry Island." There they went camping, and—— But I will let you read it for yourselves.

"Freddie! oh, Freddie!" called Flossie, coming into the house one day about a month after they had come back from New York. "Where are you, Freddie?"

"I'm out in the kitchen gettin' some bread an' jam," he answered. "What d'you want?"

"Lucy Turner is with me," went on Flossie. "She says we haven't got any bugs that go around and around and around, and I want to show her. We have got 'em, haven't we, Freddie?"

"Course we have. I've got one now going around and around and around my plate that had bread and jam on it—but there isn't any on it now, 'cause I ate it all up!"

"Oh, come on and we'll get some, too!" cried Flossie, and she and her little girl playmate were soon having fun with Freddie. And there we will take leave of them.

THE END